The m... lush summer landscape in silver and white.

Spellbound, Beck stared down at the town, swallowing over the lump that had suddenly formed in his throat.

Home.

No. He fought against the feelings that had seized him. Shared Ground was no longer his home.

And yet, there was something here he couldn't deny, something that tugged at him. Here lay the source of his spirit.

Desperately, he tried to shake off the emotions. He wouldn't allow this place to get a grip on him. He couldn't.

His gaze slid lightly across the heart of Shared Ground, searching for the garden, touching down gingerly. It was as if he were testing a wound for tenderness, afraid to settle his gaze too firmly on the spot. There.

He inhaled deeply and then searched further, looking for the house where he'd lived for the first seventeen years of his life.

He stared for a long time at the lonely light in the window far below.

Dear Reader,

When two people fall in love, the world is suddenly new and exciting, and it's that same excitement we bring to you in Silhouette Intimate Moments. These are stories with scope and grandeur. The characters lead lives we all dream of, and everything they do reflects the wonder of being in love.

Longer and more sensuous than most romances, Silhouette Intimate Moments novels take you away from everyday life and let you share the magic of love. Adventure, glamour, drama, even suspense— these are the passwords that let you into a world where love has a power beyond the ordinary, where the best authors in the field today create stories of love and commitment that will stay with you always.

In coming months look for novels by your favorite authors: Nora Roberts, Heather Graham Pozzessere, Emilie Richards and Kathleen Eagle, to name just a few. And whenever you buy books, look for all the Silhouette Intimate Moments, love stories *for* today's woman *by* today's woman.

Leslie J. Wainger
Senior Editor and Editorial Coordinator

MARION SMITH COLLINS

Shared Ground

SILHOUETTE·INTIMATE·MOMENTS®
Published by Silhouette Books New York

America's Publisher of Contemporary Romance

SILHOUETTE BOOKS
300 East 42nd St., New York, N.Y. 10017

SHARED GROUND

ISBN: 0-373-07383-6

First Silhouette Books printing May 1991

Printed in the U.S.A.

Books by Marion Smith Collins

Silhouette Intimate Moments

Another Chance #179
Better Than Ever #252
Catch of the Day #320
Shared Ground #383

Silhouette Romance

Home To Stay #773

MARION SMITH COLLINS

has written nonfiction for years, but only recently has she tried her hand at novels. She is already the author of several contemporary romances and has no plans ever to stop.

She's a devoted traveler and has been to places as far-flung as Rome and Tahiti. Her favorite country for exploring, however, is the United States because, she says, it has everything.

In addition, she is a wife and the mother of two children. She has been a public-relations director, and her love of art inspired her to run a combination gallery and restaurant for several years.

She lives with her husband of thirty years in Georgia.

Chapter 1

The black limousine, enigmatic with its shadowed windows, was parked at an angle to the curb. The tall, grim-faced man who emerged from the executive entrance to the White House didn't break stride as he walked toward the vehicle.

As a matter of course, he never waited for his driver to open the car door for him, either; but tonight his hands were full, and before he could juggle his briefcase and the extra files he carried, the driver jumped out. He nodded at the man. "Thanks, Danny," he said crisply. In one smooth movement, he ducked his head, climbed into the back seat and settled against the plush cushions.

But he didn't relax.

He seldom did. And right now, in particular, relaxation would have been impossible for Beck Mac-Domhall. He was in a black mood, despondent and frustrated as hell. His quick mind boiled, searching for alternatives to the bleak picture he saw ahead, but nothing—zero, zilch—developed.

His briefcase, locked and secure on the floor at his feet, contained only a few of the files he had to study tonight, the top-secret ones. The remainder were in an untidy pile on the seat beside him, to be scanned during the half-hour's commute to his home in suburban Virginia.

But none of the files, classified or not, could compare in importance to the worry he faced or to the loss his country was about to suffer.

Beck was cold just thinking about it. There had to be an alternative to the action his boss was contemplating. There had to be another answer, another way.

His boss was the president of the United States of America, and the man was planning to resign his position at the end of the month.

Danny got in behind the wheel, started the car, moved a few feet and then put on the brakes with enough force to send one of Beck's files sliding to the floor. He cursed under his breath. "Sorry, sir."

If Beck had not been feeling so dismal, he would have chuckled not only at the scene in front of the limo but also Danny's reaction to it.

Danny White took his assignment as Beck's driver very seriously. The young man hated anything that interfered with the smooth performance of his duty. Someone needed to tell the newly appointed secretary of transportation to move away from the driveway to hold his impromptu news conference.

Beck smiled slightly and shook his head. "Not your fault, Danny."

Actually Beck didn't object to the delay. His life had two speeds, full and flat-out. "Dead stop" was rare enough to be welcome. With the door closed, the soft purr of the engine was the only sound.

He took off his glasses and pinched the inner corners of his tired eyes. He needed to have his glasses changed. But when did he have time for something as easily post-ponable as an eye exam? He replaced the glasses, seat-ing the nosepiece firmly, and reached for the top file, ignoring the slight blurring of the title.

The muted daylight coming into the limousine over his shoulder was a welcome change; it wasn't often that he left the White House before total darkness had settled on the city. The thought made him pause and glance at his watch with a frown. Daylight? At seven-thirty? Good Lord, it was almost the middle of June.

He gave a heavy sigh—daylight savings time had ar-rived a couple of months ago, and he'd hardly noticed. He let the file drop to his lap and his thoughts roam aimlessly for a few minutes.

Added to his concern and sorrow for his boss and the country—as if that weren't enough—he had been feel-ing another, more inexplicable sense of disquiet for the past few days, this on a personal level. A premonition of a private disaster that wouldn't go away.

He'd always had a highly developed intuitive sense that had served him well, off and on through the years. Though for the most part, he tried to stifle intuition, choosing instead to depend on his own intelligence and reason, more often than not his hunches had proven true. And so he'd learned not to dismiss the sensation, and especially not when it persisted.

He had no idea what had prompted the current, crazy foreboding that had been hanging over his head, but right now he definitely didn't have the time to analyze it.

Beck's unflappable demeanor was his greatest value as special assistant to the president, who maintained that with the proper utilization of time, intelligence and effort, every problem had a solution. In this case the president's impending resignation was the problem; the solution, Beck feared, was beyond the capacities of a mere mortal to accomplish.

In the meantime, while he waited for the president's announcement, Beck's daily responsibilities, which would have swamped a lesser man, didn't cease. When you were a special assistant, you didn't waste a minute of your waking life. That was the justification for his acceptance when, immediately after his inauguration, the president insisted Beck have a driver at his disposal.

Beck would have preferred to drive himself and, God knows, *not* in a limo.

At last, the transportation secretary waved off the reporters, who dispersed quickly. Danny accelerated, made the sweep around the curved driveway, and headed toward the tall, wrought-iron gates.

The crowd that inevitably congregated just outside the grounds of the White House was more sparse than usual this evening, and quieter, made up of people easily recognized as tourists. There were no placards, no angry faces. They seemed merely curious, as people often were about the comings and goings from this place. Beck took this as a positive sign that the country had managed to muddle along fairly well. For today, at least.

He didn't know what drew his gaze to the center of the small crowd. On any other day he would have been totally immersed in one of the ever-present files within seconds of entering the car.

However, as though guided by an inner voice or pulled by a puppeteer's string, his head swiveled. He scanned the faces intently, until he met, head-on, the gaze of a tall and strikingly beautiful young woman.

He stared, holding his body rigid and motionless, like an animal sensing danger. Only one very brief rational thought flew through his mind—no one outside the car could actually see anything more than a shape behind the heavily tinted windows—and then all judicious logic vanished, taking his reason with it.

Here, in the flesh, was the explanation for his earlier premonition of personal disaster and the shadow of foreboding that had hung over him.

Her beauty would have been remarkable in any gathering, and she appeared peculiarly out of place amidst the more pedestrian contingent of tourists. She was visibly anxious; tension was evident in every line of her body. She might not be able to see inside the car, but, unquestionably, she was willing him to respond to her presence. Then, as he stared at her she seemed to feel his gaze upon her, seemed to unwind slightly, her tension ebbing. Her lips curved upward slightly in an expression of relief.

He would have known her anywhere, even without the necklace she wore. His gaze was drawn to it against his will. Damn.

From a fine gold thread around her neck, hung a golden disk, small, only about an inch in diameter. Unconsciously he reached into his pocket; her disk was a duplicate to the one he now held in his hand. Set in the center was a transparent shaving of an ancient grayish stone that looked very much like ordinary granite. The unique piece, as far as he knew, was common as grass in only one spot on this planet.

And, though the beautiful woman stood too far away for him to distinguish the color of her eyes, he knew they were emerald green. Cat's eyes.

"Stop."

The driver touched the brakes automatically, not stopping, but slowing the speed of the limo. "Sir?"

Beck, coming alive with an aggressive attack of energy, already had the door open. He offered no explanation as he stepped out of the car.

The crowd parted readily before his purposeful approach. In two strides he was beside the woman, his eyes narrowed in furious disbelief. "Cat? Catriona?" he said in a voice that didn't sound at all like his own.

The people around her, recouping now, pressed forward to see what had prompted this diversion. Ordinary crowd sounds increased to a definite buzz, like bees, hungry to take a scrap of honeyed gossip back home to Iowa or Arkansas. "Who is that?" "Don't you know? That's the president's right-hand man!"

Cat smiled the killer smile that he remembered so well and held out her hand. "Hello, Beck," she said, as though they'd last met day before yesterday instead of seventeen years ago.

Without thinking, he took her hand. His reaction to the contact of their palms was instant and electric, like a bolt of heat lightning. The sensation stunned him. For a moment he found himself at a loss, an unsettling condition and one that rarely could be applied to Beck MacDomhall. He quickly released her.

At that moment, Cat was jostled from the back, thrusting her a step closer, almost into his arms. Distress clouded her eyes. Crowds had always bothered her. She looked to him in silent appeal.

The exchange had taken only seconds, and suddenly, from the corner of his eye, Beck saw Danny shift the car into park and open the door. Beck muttered an obscenity as the young man emerged on the run, his expression forbidding, his hand reaching inside his jacket. Simultaneously one of the guards at the gate also started forward.

Beck didn't hesitate; he raised his arm to wave off his driver and the guard, grabbed Cat's elbow, and hustled her unceremoniously through the crowd and into the back seat of the limo. He climbed in after her and slammed the door. "Okay, Danny, let's go," he said, reluctantly admiring the way she had kept her composure while being manhandled into the car. She scooted the file folders into a pile to make room for herself on the seat.

When the limo had pulled free of the White House surroundings and was positioned comfortably in the flow of traffic, he finally let himself take a good look at her. He realized that there was something much more than beauty to the adult Catriona Muir.

Her sun-streaked blond hair was slicked back into a sophisticated chignon, revealing her captivating features—high cheekbones, wide forehead, tilted eyes, and that mouth, that seductive mouth—in stark relief that would have been unkind to most women. Her fair skin was flawless; her only makeup seemed to be a tinge of color on her cheeks and lashes. Or was the blush natural? Were those fatally long lashes her own? She wore a conservative black dress of simple design in some soft fabric. Her legs, crossed at the knee, were long and lovely.

As a package, Catriona Muir was understated but spectacular. Seventeen years ago, when he'd last seen

her, the promise of height had been there, certainly; but
her magnificent feminine shape had not even been hinted
of. The most lingering and familiar characteristics of the
twelve-year-old were the green of her eyes and, of
course, the killer smile.

Fully aware of his scrutiny, she raised her hand to
finger the golden disk. It was the only outward sign that
she was still nervous and uncomfortable.

Now, as he studied her, he was unexpectedly struck by
the most remarkable phenomenon. Sudden flashing
mental images of her, one superimposed over the next,
filled his senses until, at last, all the earlier stages faded
into the woman next to him. He was watching Catriona
Muir grow up—from gawky twelve-year-old child to the
beautiful woman she had become. It was as though, in
this intuitive fantasy, he was witnessing every phase of
her growth and development, both physical and emotional.

And there was something else. In each phase he identified the shadow that had always haunted her eyes. The
shadow had grown dimmer with maturity. But it remained.

He was an unwilling witness to this bizarre visual ev-
olution, but he'd had no warning, thus no time to build
his defenses against the experience. It was eerie. But it
didn't surprise him.

Mentally he shook himself.

Crazy, he told himself.

"Now, Cat, do you want to tell me what the *hell* you
are doing here?" he demanded in a low angry tone that
deepened the shadow. He cursed himself for that.

Catriona hesitated, stung by Beck's harshness, and
searched his grim expression. She observed the hard
jump of muscle in his jaw with a skeptical eye and

frowned. His anger was out of proportion to her mere presence, she told herself. Would her being here provoke questions about his background? Questions he didn't want to answer?

She wondered how thoroughly the Secret Service, or the FBI, or whoever took care of such things, had checked into Beck's family. She wondered what the official investigation had revealed about his background.

She wondered, too, if Beck had felt the sudden flash of heat when their hands had met. She would have to examine that reaction more carefully at her leisure; perhaps she could use his response to help accomplish her goal. *Something* had certainly prompted him to drop her hand so quickly, but it could have been merely a case of annoyance or irritation at seeing her where he least expected.

Because that was uppermost in her mind—to do as she had been instructed, straightaway—and then to get out of here. To go home, go back to where she belonged. She wasn't comfortable in Washington; she wasn't really comfortable anywhere except Shared Ground.

Right now, however, she had to tamp down her own resentment, not only at his unprovoked animosity but also at the necessity for this quickly planned trip.

Barely missing a beat, she met his gaze and lifted a brow. It was a gesture she had deliberately perfected, one which often came in handy when she had to deal with a jerk. "It's nice to see you again, too, Beck," she answered mildly. "You're looking well."

That was an understatement; he looked fantastic. Taller than he'd been when she last saw him, healthy, strong, he was the picture of a powerful man in his prime. He had towered over her when they'd stood together in the crowd, and she wasn't a short person. His shoulders had blocked her view. The fine tailoring defined their strength. His tanned features wore a rugged, outdoors imprint.

His unforgettable gray eyes were bracketed by lines caused by heavy responsibility and, if she wasn't mistaken, eyestrain. His dark hair had silvered at the temples. But those things only added to his inherent distinction, a distinction he shared with his ancestors.

"Catriona." He drew his pronunciation of her name out until it became a threat.

"Elena sent me," she said, thinking that surely a reference to his grandmother would have a mollifying effect. But the mention didn't seem to touch him at all.

His formidable expression really annoyed her. Who the hell did he think he was? She looked at him. "Elena thought that since we were such good friends when we were children, I might be able to convince you to return to Shared Ground for a visit," she went on, determined not to appear conciliatory.

Beck noted the lift of Cat's haughty brow and tried to remember the child she'd been. But that image had been completely obliterated by the woman she was now. He muttered a word he hadn't learned at his grandmother's knee and looked forward at the back of his driver's head. He took his glasses off and massaged his eyes.

Catriona waited with the patience she had learned so dearly through the years. Patience didn't come naturally to her. She'd been right about the strained eyes, though.

Finally, grudgingly, Beck returned his attention to her. "How is Elena?" he asked with reluctance.

Catriona followed his gaze to the driver and noted the tightness across the man's shoulders. "She's fit," she said casually. "In fact for a lady approaching one hundred, Elena is remarkable.'' She shot him a sideways glance. ''She's hoping you'll be there for her birthday.''

''That's impossible.''

Catriona's eyes narrowed, but she continued in the same noncommittal tone, careful not to reveal a hint of sarcasm. ''Of course, we all realize what a very important man you've become, but Elena thought that even the president's chief adviser could be excused for a weekend to celebrate his grandmother's hundredth birthday.''

His lips tightened as he caught the denunciation in the words, if not the tone. ''I can't,'' he responded.

''Can't or won't?'' she demanded, instantly, forgetting the driver.

Beck shrugged. ''Take your choice,'' he said evenly. Again he glanced at Danny, who was undoubtedly listening. He could be trusted not to repeat the conversation; Beck had recruited Danny himself. The young man was loyal to the president and himself. Still, it might be a good idea to change the subject. ''When did you get to Washington?''

''Yesterday. I'm staying at the Arrowhead.''

Her response jolted him. The Arrowhead—last night he'd been there to give a speech. As he'd entered the lobby, he'd known someone was watching his progress with excessive interest, but he had chosen to ignore the itching between his shoulder blades. He'd had other, more important things on his mind.

Catriona realized he'd gone on the defensive. She'd have to counter that. ''I'd like a chance to talk to you,'' she went on, ''but if tonight isn't convenient... if you have plans for the evening and need to be rid of me, you can drop me there.''

Beck considered for a minute. Simply dropping her off at her hotel wouldn't accomplish a thing. Beck's grandmother's followers were infinitely loyal. If Elena had sent Cat to Washington with orders to bring him back to Shared Ground, Cat would give it a hell of a shot.

"I don't have any plans that can't be changed, except for work," he said, indicating the files on the seat between them with a gesture. "We'll have dinner at my place. How long are you planning to stay in Washington?" he added, aware of a certain wariness in his tone that was unacceptable. If he showed the slightest indication of weakness, she would be quick to use it to her advantage. He broke off the thought, wondering why this suddenly seemed to have become a contest of some kind.

"As long as it takes to convince you to come home."

"Ah, yes, I see. You've been sent on a mission and you won't give up until you've accomplished what you set out to do." He forced amusement into his voice—whether for the benefit of his driver or for his own benefit, he wasn't sure.

"Something like that," Catriona admitted, picking up and responding in the same amused tone. "Just so I'm back in time for the party."

Beck hardly had to search his memory for the date of his grandmother's birthday. November was months away.

His suspicion stirred. "I'm still wondering why she sent you," he reflected slowly. He let his eyes roam over her touching down lightly on her breasts, her long legs. "Aside from a few obvious reasons. You've become a beautiful woman, Cat."

Catriona swallowed her antagonism. She sat perfectly still under this second, more deliberate, inspection. She knew he was curious about her, just as she had been curious about him. It was only natural.

She'd handled her own rather dramatic response to a first glimpse of him last night. Elena had sent her to Washington, told her to stay at the Arrowhead without any explanation as to why. Catriona, of course, had followed her directions; and, of course, the morning after her arrival, there had been an announcement in the paper that Beck MacDomhall would be speaking to a group in town for a convention at the Arrowhead Hotel.

When he'd entered the lobby at eight-thirty, she'd watched from a distance. Her first impression had surprised and saddened her. She had seen hardness—in his expression, in the aggressive thrust of his jaw, the unyielding shoulders, the rigid spine. The Beck she knew seventeen years ago had not been hard.

Grieving, morose, frustrated and rebellious, but not hard.

Even from afar she'd known the moment last night when he'd sensed her presence. She'd been ready, expecting that eerie sixth sense of his to kick in, and had stepped behind a column, out of sight.

Of course, the distance had watered down some of his magnetism, and she'd had the intervening twenty-four hours to collect herself, but at least she'd been more prepared than he for this face-to-face meeting. She knew she'd changed from the child she was when he left; that was no surprise surely. "She didn't intend for me to seduce you into it, if that's what you're implying."

He chuckled. "Sorry," he said. He didn't sound sorry, but she didn't really resent his reaction.

Catriona knew that her looks were startling. They had caused problems for her in the past. Men tended to assume that because she didn't bubble and gush, she was an inaccessible ice lady. In fact she was nothing of the sort. She was rather shy, and the control she exerted was in place because of fear of revealing more of herself than she wished.

"I'm the Gardener," she told him. Her announcement was accompanied by a light shrug of her shoulders. "Provisionally, of course. Your grandmother is still effectively in charge, but even she has had to slow down a bit in deference to age."

"You?" He didn't know why the information surprised him. She'd always been a favorite of his grandmother's. Even as a youngster she'd always had the intelligence, the drive, the leadership ability. Now, in addition, she had matured into an exciting creature. It wouldn't be difficult for her to influence his grandmother's followers, especially with the backing of Elena herself.

Shared Ground, Tennessee, was an arcane community with a secret contradiction, hidden deep within the Great Smoky Mountains. And the position of leadership they called the "Gardener" was a strange one, more than mayor or judge might be in another small town, only slightly less than imperial.

The story of Shared Ground would sound familiar to any student of American history. Searching for freedom, John MacDomhall and a small band of followers had left the smoldering unrest and economic distress in their Highland homeland in 1746.

That year, after the battle of Culloden, the clan system, which had been such a part of the Scottish heritage, was broken up by the "Bloody" Duke of

Cumberland. Their estates were confiscated; they were prohibited from carrying arms and forbidden to wear the tartan. And so, like millions of other emigrants, they came to America. They settled just over the border from North Carolina, deep within the Great Smoky Mountains.

The physic garden, which had been a part of their community in Scotland, was transported and, through the years, had been expanded by his ancestors. Life in Shared Ground had always existed because of the garden from which it had drawn its name.

Suddenly he was jolted by a repeat of the experience, the animallike vigilance he'd felt when he first saw Cat standing in the middle of the tourist crowd.

Suddenly he feared the woman beside him with a visceral emotion that burned his abdomen. Even were he able to ignore her beauty, set aside their history, Catriona Muir could be a magnet, drawing him back to Shared Ground, the place he'd left, without regret, years ago.

Already he was being reminded of things best forgotten. Primeval forests, majestic mountains, smoky blue-gray mist—cool in the early-morning light, clinging longest in the deep valleys. And the physic garden, the beautiful, fragrant garden with its many varied plants, some of which were survivors of ones brought from Scotland over two hundred and fifty years ago.

Flashes of memory—playing in the garden as a child while his mother and father worked nearby, gathering the herbs and spices, the elusive ginseng root. Preparing the acres for cultivation, the "simples," the home remedies, in the way they had been prepared for hundreds of years. With love and infinite care. A place of traditions. A place of quiet beauty. Peace.

No, he silently resisted, rejecting the images, the memories. Heeding the siren call of Shared Ground was a trap that he had steadfastly avoided for years. The community and its inhabitants were no longer a part of his life.

Catriona watched Beck reinforce a defense against his own memories with a certain sympathy. The transformation of his attitude—from doubtful to curious to responsive—was written plainly on his face, as easy to read as a first-grade primer. And lasted about as long as it would take to read; then came the denial.

She watched alertly. She would have to reevaluate her strategy if her quest had any chance of success. What lever should she use to get him to agree to return to Shared Ground? What lever *could* she use?

His life was obviously going well. He was a man of power, extraordinarily masculine, in charge of himself and his surroundings. He wouldn't be easy to influence.

Then she remembered his initial anger, when he'd demanded to know what she was doing here. Maybe over dinner she could analyze that reaction, learn what had provoked it. Maybe she could use it against him. She would just have to be patient. "Thank you. Dinner sounds nice." She smiled, her eyes teasing him. "Don't tell me you're going to cook it."

"No. I have a housekeeper." He gave a distracted look at his watch. "He goes home at seven, but he always leaves a meal in the oven." Something about his tone informed her that he had finished talking for now.

Catriona nodded and settled back against the luxurious cushions. She occupied herself by looking curiously around the interior of the car. She'd never ridden in a limousine before. There were two telephones and a dozen buttons on the armrest beside her. Some of them probably were remote controls for the small television. The traffic had eased and they were moving along at quite a clip, but she supposed the limousine was recognizable to the police cars they passed, because no one stopped them.

Soon the car began to slow, made a couple of turns and halted before a wrought-iron, spear-topped gate in a curved brick wall. The driver accelerated again as the gates swung inward. Around the curve of a driveway, Catriona saw a lovely town house. Of the Federalist period, its mellowed brick facade was a rosy color in the fading twilight. The mature plantings, boxwood and holly predominantly, gave the impression of having been here for as long as the country had.

The driver applied the brakes. The limo came to a gentle stop. Beck gathered up the file folders and his briefcase in one hand and opened the car doors. "Thanks, Danny," he said as he climbed out.

Catriona didn't wait for him to come around to open the door for her. This was no social visit. She joined him as he was saying a last word to the driver.

The car moved off, back down the driveway, and they mounted the front steps. Beck unlocked the door and entered first, flipping on lights to illuminate a grand entrance hall.

Directly in front of Catriona, a sweeping curved staircase rose from the shining hardwood floors like a soaring bird. The wonderful clean scent of beeswax was powerful, but even had she not smelled it, its use was evidenced by the gleaming surfaces of the tables, the hand-turned banisters and the carved newel post. To her left, she could see a dining room, and to her right, a section of a living room was visible. Everything was very formal, very correct and very beautiful.

Beck picked up a stack of mail and message slips from a hall table and flipped another switch, which activated an exquisite pair of lamps on either side of the fireplace in the living room.

He gestured for her to enter. "Have a seat. I'll get rid of these files and bring some ice." Without waiting for a response, he disappeared into the shadows beneath the staircase.

Catriona was grateful for a minute alone. She knew that he was going to be difficult the moment he directed her into this room. She supposed it should properly be called a drawing room. In any event "living" was as colossal a misnomer as she could imagine. She dropped her small purse onto a chair, inhaled deeply and exhaled on a sigh. Arms akimbo, she stood looking around her. The room was a monument to formality, dignity and status—but as impersonal and unused as a museum display.

Clearly this was not where Beck normally relaxed at the end of a long, busy day. No one could relax in here. She wondered where he would have taken her had she been an invited guest. Did he have a den on the back side of the house? It probably looked out onto a garden. She longed to see a garden again, even a city garden.

Without hesitation she followed the direction he'd taken. It took only a moment to find the room from which light spilled onto the carpeted floor of the hall. Her footsteps were muffled. She approached the door and paused, silently studying him.

Beck stood behind a desk, riffling through the stack of message slips. He'd discarded his jacket, loosened his tie and opened the top button of his white shirt. He seemed even larger, his shoulders broader without the formality of his jacket. A lock of his dark hair had fallen forward, and he pushed it back with an absent gesture. His hand remained to massage the back of his neck.

The files were stacked on the desk. There was no sign of the briefcase. She supposed he had a safe in the room. She was startled when he spoke.

"Come in," he said without looking up. His voice was clipped. "Sorry to keep you waiting." He divided the slips into two piles, dropping one pile onto the desk. The others he held, frowning down at them.

"If you need to return your calls . . ." She waved her hand and thought . . . *what shall I say? That I'll leave? That I'll wait in that awful room?* "I know my way around a kitchen fairly well." She made the statement a question to show him that she wasn't being pushy.

At that, he looked at her. Just looked at her.

And under the power and charisma of that gaze her knees were suddenly weakened, her breath arrested somewhere between her lungs and her throat. She tried to smile.

He seemed to consider her offer. "If you wouldn't mind," he answered politely. "I should take care of one or two of these."

"Certainly." She reached for the doorknob. "You probably want privacy. Shall I close the door?"

He studied her for another brief interval. Then he gave a short nod. "Please. Can you find your way? If you'd like a drink . . ."

She waved away the suggestion. "Don't worry about me." She closed the door and leaned against it for a minute to catch her breath.

It had been fairly easy to hold her own against the urbane man in the limo, but relaxed in his own setting, he was far too compelling, much too potent.

Keep your mind on what you're here for, she scolded herself.

She found the kitchen exactly where a kitchen ought to be and began nosing around. The room was white, all white, and almost painfully neat; even the pantry seemed to be arranged in alphabetical order. In the refrigerator, bottles stood in descending height. No leftovers here to clutter the shelves. Even the casserole in the oven sat precisely in the center of the oven, its square sides exactly parallel to the oven walls. His housekeeper was a man, he'd said. She smiled to herself and shook her head.

Forty-five minutes later, Catriona was sitting at the large trestle table that could have seated eight. She had found place mats and napkins and set it for two, one at the head of the table, the other at a right angle.

Delicious aromas filled the kitchen. The casserole had been effectively disguised with buttered and toasted bread crumbs, so she was trying to identify the contents by the smell of herbs. Oregano. Bay leaf. Something Italian, she decided.

She had made a salad from crisp greens and plump white mushrooms and tossed with a vinaigrette dressing before dividing it and serving it in individual wooden salad bowls. Added to the aroma of the food was the smell of freshly ground coffee brewing. She was nursing a glass of fine Bordeaux when Beck entered the room.

The loosened tie had been discarded altogether; his sleeves had been rolled back to reveal muscular forearms. She was struck anew by the power of his masculinity. But his brow was drawn with more worry lines. At the sight of her he started—as though he'd forgotten she was there, and now that he remembered, he was less than pleased.

"I'm sorry that took so long. Did you find everything you wanted?" he asked.

"Of course. I just looked under *E* for every," she quipped.

"What?"

"Never mind. It isn't important. Shall I pour you a glass of wine? It's delicious, by the way."

"No, thanks." He shook his head as he picked up the bottle and turned it in his big hand until the label faced out. "Yes. A gift from the French ambassador. I'm glad you like it."

He was talking distractedly to fill the silence. Catriona would be willing to wager a fair amount of money that, at this very moment, he would have no idea what his last comment was. This was the time to begin prying. His response might give her a clue that would help her in her quest.

Moving with studied nonchalance, she stood. "Something is clearly bothering you, Beck. Would you rather I leave?" She knew he wanted her gone, but she also knew that diplomacy would dictate a polite answer. He didn't disappoint her.

"You may as well stay for dinner," he said. "After that, I'll have to take you back to the hotel. I have some work to do."

Her chagrin must have showed clearly on her face as she turned away. She slipped padded mitts onto her hands and opened the oven door.

He'd moved to the head of the table but he didn't sit down. "Look, Cat," he said, frowning. "I didn't *ask* you to come here."

Why did his statement hurt so much? She concentrated on getting the heavy dish out without burning herself. "That's odd," she said, proud of her steady hands, her even tone. "I thought you had."

"I meant to Washington," he bit out.

She turned from the stove, the casserole in her hands. "No, you didn't, did you? And clearly you haven't time to spare for an old friend."

His dark eyes glittered dangerously from behind the cold lenses of his glasses. She wondered if she'd gone too far.

"Stop trying to put me on the defensive, Cat. A friendly visit is not the reason for your being here and we both know it. I told you I have no intention of returning to Shared Ground, ever, not even to attend Elena's birthday party. I escaped from that life years ago."

"Escaped?" The word troubled her more than anything he'd said until now. She set the dish on a hot pad she'd placed on the table and sank into the chair. She raised her eyes to his. "Is that how you saw it? Escape from your family? Your heritage? Your people?" She cursed her voice because it shook with emotion.

He leaned forward, planting his hands flat on the table. She resisted the urge to cringe under his forceful gaze as his face filled her field of vision. The lines of weariness around his eyes, his mouth, were more pronounced than they'd been when she left him in his study. But his disposition was no less dangerous.

He spoke slowly, enunciating every word. "They are not my people. Get that through your head. If my grandmother chooses to sit in that valley like a queen reigning over her subjects, that's her privilege, but leave me out of it. She thinks I should inherit her claim to leadership?"

He straightened, shoving his hands into his trousers pockets and gave a short bark of laughter. The sound that emerged wasn't amiable *or* amused. "I may be a Scot but I've never subscribed to the theory of divine right." In the silence that followed his declaration, their gazes clashed and he didn't yield an inch.

Provoked into anger by his callous attitude, Catriona nevertheless took a deep breath. It was important that she hold her temper in check. Only a coolheaded, reasoned argument would have a chance of swaying him on this. "But, surely, Beck, a few days off for a birthday celebration..."

"That's not what Elena wants and you know it. Did you and she think that I'd forgotten her birthday is months away? She wants me back there permanently, Cat. Besides, I can't take a few days off."

"I don't believe you," she snapped, feeling the anger spring forth in her tone.

She found to her surprise that she didn't care if he heard her fury. She just didn't care anymore. The arrogance of the man was stunning. His only surviving relative...when she thought of Elena's disappointment, she wanted to cry. And she was the one who would have to break the news. "She is your grandmother, you selfish bastard, and she's going to be a hundred years old! Surely, even an important man like you—"

He laughed again. This time the sound was harsh, guttural, grief stricken. It interrupted the flow of her anger and stopped her denunciation, like water turned off at the spigot.

"You don't have any idea what you're talking about, Catriona."

She was frozen into breath-stopping silence by his tortured expression.

"Important? Me?" he went on. "I'm nothing. The president of this country is important. This one is unique, a man that comes along once in a generation if the old planet Earth is very, very lucky. He is not only a superb leader, he is impeccably honest. He is also ill. No, that isn't completely accurate."

He paused, took off his glasses again and rubbed at his eyes. When he replaced them, Catriona was startled to see moisture in his eyes. The sight wrung her heart. "Beck..." she began in a softer voice.

"Actually the man is not merely sick. He is dying," Beck finished.

Chapter 2

Dear God, thought Catriona. No wonder Beck was so crushed, so devastated. The president of the United States was fatally ill.

His astonishing announcement made Catriona feel sick. She touched her throat with a shaking hand. The adrenaline that had her geared up for this confrontation had evaporated completely, leaving her numb and speechless.

Wisely she remained so.

Beck pulled out his chair and sank into it, the picture of a man wilting under a dreadful weight. He planted his elbows on the table and dropped his face into his hands.

The coffee maker gave its last gasp into the silence. Hoping that activity might calm her lurching stomach, Catriona stood and crossed to the counter. She took cups and saucers from the cabinet. She seemed to be moving in slow motion. Her breathing was shallow and the nausea persisted. A few minutes ago the delicious scents that filled the room had been tempting; now they were too heavy, too rich. Finally she flattened her hands on the cool counter tiles and let her head fall forward.

Beck had called the president unique, and she knew that to be the truth. He was the source of hope for millions of people who had grown disillusioned and frustrated over many of the problems of the world in general and their country in particular. He'd been in office for less than two years, but already the atmosphere in the nation's cities was improved. Integrity had become an acceptable word again. Pride was slowly being restored.

Shared Ground might be an isolated community hidden deep in the mountains of Tennessee, but the people of the community were fully aware of the stature of the man who presently lived in the White House.

She straightened, finished pouring the coffee and placed one cup in front of Beck and another at the place she'd set for herself.

He turned his head. "Thank you," he said quietly.

She glimpsed his expression from a new angle and was surprised to see he'd recovered his control and balance quickly. The moisture in his gray eyes had been replaced by a glint of steel, and determination hardened his jaw. She began, cautiously, to hope again. If anything could be done, Beck would see that it *was* done.

She returned to the counter for sugar and cream and took her seat. They served themselves from the steaming casserole, and she picked up her fork. Unable to swallow, she laid it down again. "What's the matter with the president?"

He shrugged. "As far as I can gather in layman's language, some of the glands in his body have ceased to function as they are supposed to do. The worst effect is on the adrenals and the pancreas. He's so hyperactive that he barely sleeps. Exhaustion overtakes him for a while, then it starts all over again."

Catriona bit off a sigh of despair. "Beck, despite your alienation, it is a point of honor to Elena that her grandson is an adviser to a man like the president. She—we all respect him tremendously. I'm sorry that I was sarcastic about your important position."

He looked up. His smoky-gray eyes were clouded again. If he was surprised by her apology, his expression didn't reveal it. "I told you before, Cat, I'm not the important one."

He sounded infinitely tired. She bit at her lower lip and smiled slightly. "To your grandmother, you are very important." She paused, wondering if she changed the subject... "Tell me, Beck, how did you link up with the president?"

Beck put down his fork and shoved his plate aside. He crossed his arms on the table in front of him. His eyes sought a point in the middle distance. "I was in St. Louis on business during his campaign for governor of Missouri. Something about the man drew me...a look in his eyes, a ring of sincerity in his voice..." He shrugged. "I'm not sure what it was. Anyway, he interested me. I went down to his headquarters to pick up some literature. He happened to be there that day. We talked for a few minutes and then he had to leave...a speech to make. He asked me to go along. The rest is, as they say, history. Before the day was over he'd offered me a job and I'd accepted."

"Did you have trouble with security clearance?"

Her question drew his gaze. He smiled. "Of course not. Shared Ground is just a small town in Tennessee." He paused and then asked, "Is Elena really well?"

The question was the first suggestion of personal curiosity he'd shown. She was grateful that they seemed to have passed a hurdle of some kind. "She really is." Catriona's eyes sparkled for a minute with the thought of the wonderful woman who held the community together. "There have been a lot of changes in Shared Ground." She very nearly blushed at the understatement, but she wouldn't go into it right now. "But the garden is as beautiful as it always is in the summer, and the community is thriving, as well."

"You know it can't last forever. I'm surprised something hasn't happened before now."

Catriona's smile became puzzled. "I don't know what you mean."

He lifted his shoulders. "You know, a community, a cult like Shared Ground, will eventually die. The community will either wither from within or succumb to outside influences. The world is too small for it to survive much longer."

She shrank from the observation, then squared her shoulders, going on the offensive. "We've survived for nearly three hundred years," she reminded him. "And I don't like your use of the word *cult*. It connotates some kind of slavery to an ideal. Our people are not slaves."

"*I* felt like one."

She inhaled sharply, but she managed to keep her voice level. He didn't need another unpleasant argument right now, but she couldn't let it pass, either. "If you felt that way, the feeling had to come from within yourself, Beck. When you left, did storm troopers come after you to drag you home in chains? Has anyone ever tried to convince you to return before this?"

"There are other kinds of chains. My grandmother knew right where I was all the time, didn't she? For the last seventeen years I've been checked up on regularly. Did she think I wouldn't notice? When I was in college I'd turn a corner or come out of a building to see a member of the community. I never knew when I'd run into one of them."

"You're talking about us like we're creatures from outer space. During the years immediately after you left, your grandmother was deeply concerned about you. You were only seventeen. The sudden death of your parents, your running away—she was very worried."

He went on as though Cat hadn't spoken. "Then when I came to Washington with the president— Bill Campbell was the last one she sent. It was about a year ago. I saw him in a crowd of tourists at the opening of Congress. And you. I didn't see you, but you were in the lobby of the hotel last night, weren't you?"

She nodded. "And I knew you were aware of me. Do you still deny that you have a gift?" she asked with a raised brow.

He ignored the reference to a gift. "I've been taking care of myself for a long time now. My grandmother doesn't need to worry."

"Oh, for heaven's sake, Beck," she said impatiently. "After all you've accomplished, working your way through college, building a consequential career, and doing it all on your own. Elena knows that she doesn't have to worry anymore."

"Then why did she send you up here? And don't give me that bull about my coming home for a visit."

Catriona hesitated. Then she shrugged. There was no point in being less than honest about Elena's motives. She wasn't nearly as ready to reveal her own. "Your grandmother is hoping you might be ready to accept your responsibility to the community. She *does* hope you're ready to come home for good."

His impatience was palpable. "I don't *have* a responsibility to the community. I've been gone from there for seventeen years. Those people don't even *know* me, for God's sake."

"They still consider you their designated leader. Even now, when the community is threatened by your—" Catriona searched her mind for a word and came up with the wrong one "—abdication."

"Abdication?" His impatience gave way to anger. He interrupted with a slash of his hand through the air. "Good God, Cat! You make Shared Ground sound like some kind of damned antiquated kingdom. This is America, not sixteenth-century Scotland."

Her indignation flowered. "Certainly it is America. The people of Shared Ground follow the laws of this country as they have done since they emigrated. You know how the quotation on the base of John Mac-Domhall's statue reads," she said, naming his ancestor, the man who had led the small band of Scots to the remote mountain community.

Tight-lipped, he nodded. " 'Speak to the earth of this virgin land and let it teach you anew of the wisdom of the centuries,' " he repeated.

"Those people were brave. They came with a dream of new customs and new loyalty to a new country. And nearly three hundred years later, a lot of new things are still going on in Shared Ground." If he only knew! "But the community has retained the old ways, too, and there's nothing wrong with that. It has given us a lot of advantages, advantages that are really exciting. Why we even have…" Her voice trailed off as he stood abruptly. He swung his gaze to glare at her and then turned away.

"I really don't want to hear it." He unplugged the coffeepot, brought it to the table and topped off their cups. A muscle jumped in his jaw.

"Why not?" she demanded.

He raised the cup to his lips and watched her over the rim. He seemed to have settled down. After a minute he spoke again. "Listen to me carefully, Cat. If the community weren't so isolated, it would have been assimilated years ago. It's only a matter of time and geography."

She resented his thinking this was a foregone conclusion. He was wrong and it angered her that he was blind to the faults of his reasoning. "It's a matter of tradition and trust," she snapped. "It's a matter of having confidence in leaders who have never before let the community down." She took a breath and blurted out, "Not until you."

"Sit down."

She hadn't realized that she'd half risen out of her chair. She sat back down and tried again for control. "You know, Beck, when Elena requested that I come to you, I was angry because I couldn't say no to her. For years I've strived to live up to what she expected of me."

"Because you're grateful. Your whole life shouldn't be dictated by gratitude. God, Cat, you could leave."

"I don't want to leave. I don't even like to leave for brief periods like this trip. I feel very lucky to be a part of—"

"Lucky?" he interrupted. "Lucky that your mother happened to die in a back country hospital in the Smokies, leaving a small child with a community of strangers, that no one in the community was brave enough to go out with you, to help you find your real family? That they decided just to keep you?"

She closed her eyes for a minute. "My mother asked them to take care of me."

He spoke the truth, or as much of the truth as he was privy to. He had no idea that she had traced her family and found out some rather depressing things. "Take it as a given, Beck, that I'm more than content. I've acted as Gardener, with Elena's help of course, for a number of years now. But, nonetheless, I've been rated second to someone who walked away from our life without a backward look." She took a deep breath, wondering if this was the time for complete candor.

She was torn by this assignment she'd been handed, and Elena had known it. Now Beck would know it, as well. For the good of the community, she'd hoped to convince him to return for at least long enough to reconcile his differences with his grandmother.

But, contrary to what he thought, and contrary to Elena's wishes, she *wanted* his return to be temporary. She wanted the job of Gardener for herself. "I suppose I should give you fair warning. To be honest, Beck, my goal is to usurp your place."

Beck's reaction puzzled her. She'd expected more derision or ridicule. Instead he gave a humorless chuckle and said offhandedly, "You're welcome to my place, Cat. You will make a perfect Gardener—intelligent, dedicated, and loyal to the community."

"You make me sound like a faithful hound," she grumbled, only slightly appeased.

This time when he laughed softly, there was real amusement in the sound and his expression lost some of its harshness.

Their eyes met and held for a moment. Beck was the first to withdraw his gaze. "Tell me more about yourself, Cat." He looked up again, briefly. "I always felt that we were close, but it's been a long time. How old were you when I left? Twelve? Or thirteen?"

"Twelve." She hesitated. "I felt close to you, too, Beck. You were the only one I could talk to." Her voice was very soft when she added, "I've missed you."

"Is there a man in your life?" he asked.

She was glad he'd looked away. After the rather powerful response she'd had to him, she was sure she was flushed. "Not really. Not lately."

"Did you leave the community?"

It was a rhetorical question. With very few exceptions all the inhabitants of the isolated village left, at least briefly, for their education.

They were encouraged to do so, to travel, to learn, and return to the community and share their knowledge. The policy had always been the basis, the foundation for progress in Shared Ground.

"I went to college of course. Georgetown."

"Georgetown?" So close? Beck was surprised, but then he shook his head, answering his own unspoken question. "No, I would still have been in Missouri then. What did you study?"

"I have an undergraduate degree in botany and a degree in law."

He was surprised by the second. Then he nodded slowly. "Good choice. Elena could augment your education with everything else you needed to know about the garden, but a knowledge of the law and justice would be essential for the Gardener."

"Especially one who will always be lacking." She didn't need to elaborate. She wasn't a direct Mac-Domhall descendant and didn't have the accompanying peculiarity that distinguished the line. "The people of Shared Ground are fully aware that I don't have the family's incredible gift. They'll never give me their total allegiance," she said.

Beck was amazed by such a matter-of-fact observation. "Oh, come on, Cat. You're an educated woman. Do you really believe that nonsense?"

Catriona traced the place mat with her fingernail. When she spoke, her voice was reserved. "For a long time I thought it was nonsense, too. But her talent— whatever you want to call it, ESP, sixth sense, second sight—is very real and very effective. I've been a witness to it many times."

"She has highly developed instincts, or especially keen intuition, take your choice," he said warily. "It's a talent, or something similar, but there certainly isn't anything magical about it."

She shook her head vehemently. "Elena's powers go far beyond mere talent, Beck. And yours do, too."

At that he straightened. "Nonsense. You've lived all your life with a clan of superstitious Scots. I know you feel that they've been good to you, but you ought to know better than to endow them with supernatural powers."

"Not all of them, Beck. Just the MacDomhalls."

She could understand Beck's doubts; she'd had them, too. She leaned forward in her urgency to have him understand. "Regardless of your feelings about the subject, I don't know how you can deny that there's a certain enchantment about Shared Ground. How many other villages in this country do you know where they've never had a murder, or a rape? How many don't have a drug problem?"

"If things are going so well, why are you here? And why now?"

The question was blunt and to the point, and she was slightly taken aback by it. The truth was, she hadn't been made privy to all the details in Elena's reasoning. But her relationship with Elena was based on mutual trust. So she hadn't questioned the older woman's direction.

Beck knew her background and her resulting lack of self-confidence. Her mother had died and left her in the mountain community when Cat was only four years old. As a child she'd never quite lost the feeling that she was an outsider. "I told you things have changed. Years ago Elena began to be concerned about the aging population. She began recruiting new people. I'm no longer the only non-Scot in Shared Ground."

"Maybe you are a Scot," he reminded.

She smiled a half smile, remembering her habit of confiding in Beck when they were children.

Often, when she was feeling particularly depressed, she would go to him, and his commonsense talk usually helped ease her sense of abandonment. When common sense didn't work, he would invent colorful scenarios in which she was a fairy child or an angel come to earth or a princess. His support helped, but she still never quite overcame the feeling of being an outcast.

It was easy to determine why she pestered Beck so much—he was a hero to her. He was the son of the Gardener. Until his father died and the position reverted back to an unwilling Elena. She would have held it only until Beck reached his twenty-first birthday. If he hadn't left the community first.

What Catriona had often wondered was why the young Beck was willing to spend so much time with her. When she was young, she had never had the nerve to ask. Now she eyed him speculatively and rested her chin in the cup of her palm. "Tell me something, Beck. I must have been an awful pest following you around like I did,'' she said. ''Why on earth did you bother with me?''

He seemed surprised by the question. ''You were a nice kid,'' he said offhandedly. ''Besides, you were from the outside. You weren't one of us. I envied that.''

Catriona winced inwardly. She supposed wearing the label of outsider all her life was responsible for what she was today, why she still worked so hard to make herself indispensable to Elena. She sighed.

Beck felt a quick stab of sympathy for this beautiful woman who had taken on a heavy burden of responsibility. She was young for the job.

He knew how the system worked. Shared Ground was a fully operational part of the United States. They couldn't very well fence it off. Occasionally people did wander in—hikers mostly. If they decided they wanted to stay, the Gardener had to approve. If they didn't have that approval, they were not expelled forcefully, they were not discriminated against, they were simply discouraged. Oh, it was done very civilly, very legally. No one had any land for sale, they found it difficult to get a job they enjoyed, they weren't quite accepted. Boredom usually drove them on.

His voice held a tinge of bitterness. ''Does the Gardener still have to countenance admitting outsiders into Shared Ground?''

''Yes.'' And that was the rub. That was the one decisive responsibility of the Gardener that Catriona was afraid of. Her fear was that she wouldn't *know*. As Elena knew, as Beck would know. Using the talent, the gift, for seeing into the heart of a person. ''Fortunately, decisions like that rarely have to be made,'' she said.

"But if that isn't a dictatorship, I don't know the definition of one."

"Anyone can leave at any time," she said defensively.

"But they can't stay unless the Gardener decides to welcome them."

"Right. And it works, too." Her mind conjured up pictures of the community. New things, exciting things were being done there. And not only in the garden. "If you could see the changes, the things we've done, the progress we've made—"

"I'm not interested in your progress. I won't be a part of the hocus-pocus. Period."

Beck could say what he wanted, she'd been a witness too many times to Elena's insight into people who wanted to join the community.

A few months ago there was a group that turned out to be less innocent than she, herself, had judged them to be. Thank goodness, Elena had stepped in.

She put the unhappy memory out of her mind. It was an occasion when her own fallibility had been demonstrated all too plainly. He'd spoken of instincts. Well, she would have to depend on instincts that were the result of training instead of genetic gifts. She knew that those simulated instincts would not always be enough. They weren't fail-safe. That fact had been demonstrated once or twice with troubling significance.

Still, what choice did the community have? If Beck refused to return, and Elena—she forced herself to think the unthinkable—died, she would have the total responsibility, including the decisions as to who was welcomed into the community and who wasn't. She'd been educated for the responsibility, and she reasoned that she could do it fairly well. That was half the battle, wasn't it?

Beck seemed to sense her doubt. "Cat, I have no regrets about leaving Shared Ground. None at all." His expression softened into an appealing half smile. "I won't go back, ever. I don't know why you would want the job, but as far as I'm concerned, it's yours."

"It is more than a job, Beck. It's—" she waved her hand, unable to think of an adequate way of expressing herself "—like a calling, sort of," she finished.

"It was unfair of Elena to use you for this," he said, after a minute.

"No." She drew the word out, her mind racing as she spoke.

Her feelings toward him were undergoing a change, and she didn't know whether she liked it or not. She was fully prepared for his antagonism on this subject or any other relating to his return. She wasn't prepared for his sympathy and understanding.

"Elena wasn't being unfair. She really had no choice. I'm her confidante, her right hand. I was the logical choice to approach you, even though seemingly the contradictory one. And I still urge you to reconsider," she said, hoping her sincerity would come through. "Although, since you've told me about the president's condition, I can understand better your reasons for resisting," she added quietly. "Clearly he needs you."

He reached across the table, took her hand, linked their fingers and cupped his other hand around hers. It was the first time he'd touched her since they shook hands outside the White House. The electricity was there, though the voltage had diminished. There was also sorrow and an odd sense of loss between them now. "Your honor and duty to the community won't let you do less than your best to persuade me. I'm impressed, Cat. You've grown into a strong, beautiful woman." He grinned. "The sensual combination alone is potent."

She opened her mouth to protest.

"But the answer is still no. Go back to Shared Ground and tell Elena you tried."

He looked into her eyes for a long, silent minute. His fingers flexed around her hand. He seemed to be about to say something else, but then the telephone rang, jarring them both.

With a sigh Beck released her hand, tilted his chair and reached back toward the wall set. "MacDomhall," he said brusquely.

The caller identified himself and Beck glanced at Cat. She understood immediately. "I'll hang up here if you want to take it in your study."

He gave her a grateful look. "Thanks."

A few minutes later, Beck hunched over his desk, the telephone receiver dangling loosely from his thumb and forefinger. Then he tightened his grip and brought the mouthpiece to his lips. "I won't accept that," he said harshly. "What about that other endocrinologist, the one from Sweden? Get him over here."

"Beck," said the White House physician in a tired voice. "The man from Sweden was here last week, don't you remember? We've had the president examined by every top physician in every field of medicine. They all agree that his illness is indefinable."

"So much for modern medicine," Beck scoffed. "I guess we'll find out what was wrong with him at the autopsy."

A heavy silence greeted his words. "That isn't fair," said the other man.

Beck could hear the sorrow and frustration in the doctor's voice. He regretted his caustic tone.

"Do you think it doesn't devastate me to watch my dearest friend losing strength every day?" the doctor went on.

Beck sighed heavily. "I'm sorry, Hal. I know you've done all you can." He paused. "He's going to resign at the end of the month."

"Beck, I'm just his doctor. I don't know all about the negotiations he is conducting, but maybe without the pressure and stress... Maybe with complete rest..." The doctor's voice trailed off.

"We both know better than that, Hal." Beck looked out through the French doors to find that it had begun to rain. He sighed. "It isn't my explanation to make, Hal, but his frustration at a breakdown of the negotiations he's conducting right now will be a heavier burden than the illness is. He'll never rest, because he'll never forgive himself," he finished.

"Then all we can do is pray," said the doctor.

Beck snorted. "Pray to who? God? Do you really think there is one?" he demanded angrily. A sudden crash of thunder echoed outside the house. The lights still burned, but the telephone had gone dead in his hand. He glanced through the window.

Sorry, said Beck to the unknown. His apology was met with a soft staccato of raindrops on the glass. *But if You* do *exist, and you are a loving God, how can You even consider taking a man like the president from us? Humanity needs this one, God. Spare him. Please.*

After a minute Beck replaced the receiver, rose and returned to the kitchen.

Catriona had cleaned away the dishes, but the room was empty. He was jolted by a swift impression that he'd dreamed the past few hours, that he'd dreamed her. Then he noticed that the back door leading to the patio was ajar. He stepped outside.

The patio was covered, but this was a gusting, blowing downpour. He paused. The smell of the rain soaking the earth, nourishing the plants, cleaning the air, filled his nostrils and soothed his inner turmoil. He looked for Cat and, when he found her, he smiled at the sight. He'd forgotten how much she loved the rain.

As his gaze narrowed in on her, however, he felt a growing sexual desire and awareness. To know her intimately, to caress the long line of her leg, to feel the weight of her breasts in his hands.

It had been so long since he'd had softness, and warmth, and beauty in his life. He tried to dismiss the desire.

And, as he'd admitted to himself earlier, this wasn't little Catriona Muir, the skinny, awkward child she'd been seventeen years ago. This was a warm, vital woman. A woman who, if he had the opportunity, he would definitely try to bed.

It was the surprise, that was all, and a natural curiosity of a normal man for a beautiful woman. But, of course, he not only wouldn't have the opportunity, he wouldn't have the time. And there were too many complications there.

She leaned against a broad square pillar at the far end of the porch. The light from the room behind him limned her shadowy figure in a soft golden glow. She looked out into the stormy night, an expression of exhilaration on her face. She wasn't soaked but she wasn't completely dry, either. The light and mist cast a grainy, luminous halo over her head. As he watched, a gust of wind picked up the hem of her dress. Absently she lowered her hand to anchor the soft fabric to her thigh. She raised her other hand to smooth her hair.

The unconsciously erotic pose turned him to stone. It defined her breasts, pushing against their confinement, her tiny waist and her impossibly long legs.

Beck's body came to life with an explosion of desire, this one not so easily dismissed. His mind rejected the sensation, but his body was immersed in a sudden, primitive urge to have her. Now. Here. With the wind and the rain howling their protest.

He wanted to go to her, to drag her into his arms and plunder her lips, those soft inviting lips that had been luring him to taste from the first moment he'd seen her.

The urge was a legacy from his less civilized ancestors, he understood wryly, but that didn't make it any less powerful.

Without saying a word, he walked purposefully toward her and stopped barely inches away, waiting for her to acknowledge his presence.

She turned her head, her smile of pleasure lingering on her lips. But when she met his gaze, she caught her breath. The smile diminished, then was gone. The hand touching her hair dropped to her side. If she had made any negative movement, any at all, he would have retreated. At least, that was what he told himself later.

But she didn't. Suddenly a flash of lightning illuminated them, as if the sun shone through the darkness for a brief, brilliant instant. It was followed seconds later by a crash of thunder. Her eyes grew huge and dark, as violent as the night, the green depths churning not with fear but with full awareness of his desire, acknowledging the inevitable milestone that was about to occur between them.

As though the thunder had been a signal, Beck planted his hands on the pillar on each side of her head and leaned down. He covered her mouth boldly, hungrily and with absolute assurance. Was it his imagination, or did she raise her mouth to his at the last second?

Catriona closed her eyes; she realized that she'd been waiting for this. Her heart began to pound with excitement and wonder. Her blood quickened. She let her head fall back under the force of his kiss to rest against the pillar. Only their lips were joined, but the effects of the emotional storm were as profound as the effects created by nature. She had become a part of the night, her entire being stirred with unexpected and violent emotions. The wind growled softly in her ear, or was that a sound from Beck?

When Beck finally lifted his head, he was breathing hard. He looked into her eyes for a long minute, his own eyes dark but guarded. She could read nothing from his expression. At last, he straightened and moved away from her. He thrust his hands into his pockets and stood gazing out into the night.

Catriona hesitated. She had come outside to enjoy the storm—to her there was nothing so glorious as the forces of nature flexing their muscles to remind man who was in charge. With the onset of the kiss, her pleasure in the rain and wind had ripened into another, more exciting pleasure, one that she had not experienced for years. The feeling was not welcome; it could only blur the outlines of her purpose here and it left her shaky, her emotions in disorder.

At last, she made a move to return to the house. Beck cleared his throat, halting her with the sound.

"I didn't mean for you to clean up the dishes," he told her, raising his voice slightly to be heard over the noise of drops hitting the roof.

Was the kiss not even to be mentioned? "You were busy. It was no trouble," she answered, searching his grim profile. "It was only a kiss, Beck," she said softly.

He turned to fix her with a stare of disbelief. "Do you believe that?"

Her gaze dropped first. He was right. It wasn't *only* a kiss. She was still unsteady from the effects.

He belonged here, she belonged in Shared Ground. There was no middle road for them, no common ground.

If this attraction developed into something complicated, they would be in deep trouble. They each had strong commitments, and their commitments were to different places, different lives and to different persons, not to each other. She paused, then went on in a softer tone. "I take it your call was more bad news."

Beck had to strain to hear. He ran a hand across the back of his neck. "It was the president's doctor. Things don't look too good," he admitted. He glanced across his shoulder. "Cat, I know I've told you a lot—"

This time it was she who interrupted him. "You don't have to worry that I'll repeat anything, Beck. I hope you realize that."

"That's right. You were trained to keep a secret, weren't you?" he answered coolly.

Catriona wasn't going to respond to his derision, not this time. She feared her wavering tone would give her away. She started for the door. "If you'll call me a taxi, I'll get out of your way."

He caught her arm as she passed. "I'll take you," he said. He tried to avoid her mesmerizing eyes—the feel of her smooth skin under his fingers was test enough—but the effort was beyond him. He wanted to kiss her again, wanted to feel those soft lips yield to his, wanted her body crushed against the length of his. He fought the urge, fought it as if he were fighting for his life.

"Beck, there's no need..." she began in a quiet, almost inaudible voice.

"I said I'll take you," he responded curtly.

Beck dropped Cat off at the hotel. Repeatedly during the drive back to his house, he told himself that he was glad to see the last of her.

Cat had changed. Almost as much as his perspective of her. After only a few hours in her company, he barely remembered the child, the good buddy, the friend. To the contrary, his lightning-fast passionate response to her sensuality was a blow to his control.

He was fully aware of his grandmother's strong moral disposition; Elena would never have sent her protégé to Washington with the aim of seducing him home, but it remained a very real danger in any case. He should never have kissed her.

If things were different, if he wasn't so distracted by the president's illness and covered up with work, he might put the memory of Cat as a child away into the past where she rightly belonged. He might have spent more time exploring the seductive potential that surrounded this intriguing woman. But, right now, he should be grateful that he was busy, because her allure definitely touched something in him that had lain dormant for a long while.

Curiously he wished also that he could have talked openly with Cat about a lot of things. He wished he could have explained exactly how vital it was that the president's negotiations continue.

The president had begun the project soon after his inauguration. He'd been able to convince, on the force of his personality alone and via secret satellite conferences, seven of the most powerful people on earth to come together informally around an electronic negotiating table.

Not all the people involved were heads of state, but each of them had profound influence on a vast section of the world's population. Some were long-time enemies. But the president had garnered statistics to convince them of the necessity of talking. He was able not only to suggest common goals but practical ways to a reasonable expectation of fulfilling those goals.

They were beginning to make progress. But the six others had indicated that they wouldn't be willing to negotiate with anyone else.

He found to his surprise that he would have enjoyed talking to Cat about the negotiations.

Catriona hated hotel rooms as much as she hated cities. She liked to be able to breathe clean mountain air; she liked to look up at the night sky and see the natural light of the stars reflected there. In a city the predominant smell was exhaust fumes, and the night sky was blurred by pollution and reflected only man-made lights.

She took off her shoes and dropped her purse onto the dresser. Then she flopped back on the bed to think. Her thoughts were muddled by the scene with Beck, by her response to his sensual appeal and by his innate masculinity, his strength, his damned hard-nosed resistance to his grandmother's wishes.

When she was at home in Shared Ground, she tended to forget about the outside. She supposed she was a victim of selective amnesia. She was happy there, among people who loved her and whom she loved. She had even come to terms with her mother's actions.

At the thought of her mother, she rolled to her stomach and squeezed her eyes shut, remembering—against her will—the pale, drawn face of Leanne, as she was the last time her daughter would ever see her.

Leanne had tried to smile as she'd bent over Catriona's cot in the community guest quarters. It was dark outside and quiet inside, and her mother spoke in a hushed whisper. "Catriona . . . sweetheart, I have to go away for a while. To the hospital." Four-year-old Catriona didn't know what a hospital was.

"You must be a good girl and wait for me," Leanne had cautioned. "This is Mrs. Muir, she is going to let you stay with her." Catriona did not know who Mrs. Muir was, either, but she had smiled tentatively at the older woman who stood behind her mother's shoulder.

"I'll be back soon," Leanne had said, giving her a last tight hug.

Perhaps if her mother had simply walked out on her, perhaps if she hadn't told her goodbye, it would have been easier. Instead, she remembered standing by the window for days, weeks, months. Her heart had suffered with each passing day. Waiting. Watching the road that climbed the side of the mountain. Hoping. Convinced that if she was a very good girl and didn't cry, her mother would return.

Long after Mrs. Muir explained what a hospital was, long after Mrs. Muir told her that her mother was dead, she remained by the window, lost in a terrible silence. When they tried to coax her away, she ignored them.

When they tried to move her forcibly, she fought like a crazy person. So they left her. And the waiting and the silence became the fundamental elements of her life.

Beck was the one who had finally brought her out of it. He talked to her even when she refused to answer. He needled her, he pestered and teased her. At last he was able to accomplish what the grown-ups, with their kindness, could not. He kept at her until, at last, she turned away from the window in anger and spit angrily at him. That was when he started calling her Cat....

Catriona caught her breath on a sob. She hadn't cried then and, by damn, she wouldn't cry now.

But thinking of Beck brought back the take-charge feel of his lips on hers; she felt again the electric excitement that had rushed through her. His mouth was exceptionally skilled in the art of kissing. Damn. She didn't need this.

In one swift movement she rolled over and surged to her feet. She strode into the bathroom and turned the cold water on full force, splashing her face over and over, until her heated cheeks cooled.

She lifted her head to look in the mirror. Well, she told herself wryly, he had certainly negated one of her assumptions tonight. He'd marked paid to her rather naive theory that since they'd been friends in the past, they could remain friends in the future. There was nothing at all friendlike about that kiss. She was no longer a girl and he was most emphatically no longer a boy.

Her eyes took on a cast that she didn't like. It was too dreamy, too sultry, too...wanton. She laughed and shook her head at her foolishness.

Pragmatic Catriona Muir had never been wanton in her life. She led a peaceful existence. She was an important member of a vital community. She lived in a modern American version of utopia. Why should she want to leave? Ever?

She fumbled for a hand towel and dried her face. She wished she could speak to Elena, but the woman refused to have a telephone installed in her home. She threw the towel aside and returned to the bedroom. She supposed she could call a neighbor, but Elena had given her specific instructions in case an unexpected situation—she supposed the president's illness would qualify as unexpected—should arise.

All she had to do was carry out Elena's directives.

Ha. Elena didn't know what Beck's reaction would be—that he would still think of Shared Ground as a clan of archaic spiritualists.

Or did she?

Elena was unaware, too, that Catriona had another, underlying motive in trying to convince Beck to return, albeit temporarily. There remained a number of things she didn't know about serving the community as Gardener. Things that, when asked, Elena would describe as ''something for another day.''

Catriona wanted to know it all. If she could somehow convince Beck to come back with her, she'd stick like glue until she discovered what Elena meant by ''another day.'' So she'd kept her questions to herself, and her motives.

Chapter 3

Catriona hadn't slept well at all. She didn't know whether to blame her insomnia on the hotel or on Beck. She was out of the tumbled bed by five o'clock and fully dressed before six.

She had chosen carefully what she'd wear—a linen suit in a conservative hunter green, a white blouse with tiny tucks sewn vertically on the bodice and a comfortable pair of pumps. As she thought about the call she had to make she paced, as she always did when she was nervous, the floor of the fifteen-by-fifteen-by-nine box.

Exactly at six she picked up the telephone. Beck's number was unlisted, as she'd learned when she had tried to contact him upon her arrival. But last night she'd memorized the number from the telephone in his kitchen.

"Hello."

He sounded awake and alert. Thank goodness, she thought with wry gratitude to providence. She wouldn't want to present this argument, her last-ditch effort, to a sleepy man. "Beck, this is Cat."

Miles away, Beck responded to the statement with a soundless groan. He should have known it wasn't going to be that easy to get rid of her. "Good morning," he said, keeping his tone noncommittal. He gripped the receiver between his shoulder and ear and started to work on the buttons of his white shirt. He was in a hurry, worried, and dreams of this woman hadn't made his short sleep very restful. He resented the frissons of warmth that her voice sent down his spine.

She went on, "I have a suggestion to make to you. Could we meet?"

He had finished buttoning his shirt and scraped his keys, his change off the dresser. He hesitated for a moment over the medallion before pocketing it. He stowed his wallet in his hip pocket and reached for his tie, a subdued burgundy paisley. Finally he answered heavily. "Cat, I don't see the point. We said all that was to be said last night. I'm not going to change my mind."

"Not about that. I have a possible solution to your other problem. You know, the—"

"I know," he interrupted before she could make any specific remarks.

"Could we meet somewhere, Beck? It's really important," she repeated.

Beck thought for a minute. Danny could probably make it into the city in thirty minutes if the traffic wasn't heavy. "I'll meet you in the park across the street from your hotel. Six-thirty."

"I'll be there."

He hung up. What the hell was she up to? He slung the tie around his neck, made quick work of a neat Windsor and reached for his jacket. He left the bedroom and took the steps two at a time, shrugging into the dark jacket of his suit as he went.

The limousine was waiting beside the front steps. "Morning, Danny," he greeted the young man as he settled the coat across his shoulders.

"Morning, sir."

"Let's hurry. I have a detour to make."

The limo arrived at the park in less than half an hour. Danny pulled the long car to the curb. "Keep the motor running and try to wait here," Beck told him as he opened the door and stepped out. "If not, circle the block. This shouldn't take long."

Catriona was pacing in the early-morning shadow of a statue of a revolutionary war patriot. Last night's rain had cleansed the city, and Beck cut across the still-damp grass toward her.

She was fresh faced and beautiful and, when she turned at his approach, her eyes were as clear as a sylvan crystal pool.

There was pleasure in the smile she gave him. "Good morning," she said affably.

"Good morning." Her necklace winked in the sunshine, provoking a restless need to hurry this up, say goodbye—again—and get to work.

He reached her side, carrying a sack with the logo of a well-known fast-food chain. "I brought us coffee and biscuits," he grumbled.

"I hadn't thought of breakfast. Thanks," she said.

Up close, she smelled like jasmine. His gaze lingered on her glossy lips, and he wondered how her mouth would taste this morning. Like fresh, minty toothpaste, probably. He begrudged her smooth brow; clearly she hadn't had any trouble sleeping.

They settled on a nearby park bench with the food between them. She opened the sack, took out a steaming cup of coffee and removed the plastic lid. She tried to sip. "Too hot to drink," she said, setting the cup on the bench. She unwrapped a plump biscuit filled with raisins and iced with sugar and took a bite.

Her movements were fluid and feminine, her long fingers, graceful. Beck watched every gesture like an enthralled teenager. A tiny bit of the sweet icing was caught in the corner of her mouth. He waited for her to remove it with her tongue and she didn't disappoint him. Then she licked some more off her index finger. He almost groaned aloud.

"Mmm, that's good," she said, smiling at him. "The only thing I miss when I'm in Shared Ground is good old junk food."

Beck quickly looked away, not commenting. He scowled as he bit off half his biscuit in one mouthful and chewed vigorously.

When he didn't answer, Catriona glanced over at him and encountered the frown. He was chewing the biscuit with as much vigor as he would use on a bite of tough steak. She wished he didn't look so darned appealing in the early light of morning. He was freshly shaved and his hair was combed neatly. Unexpectedly she remembered the taste of his kiss. Drat, it was a crime for a man to be so sexy. Even his frown was exciting.

Maybe he was one of those people who couldn't function well before breakfast. Or maybe he'd had more bad news about the president's condition.

Before she could inquire, he spoke. "Okay, Cat. What's this all about?"

While she had waited for Beck to arrive, Catriona had used the time to organize her thoughts. She was ready;

her arguments were in good order. But now, at his question, she discovered that she needed a few more moments to bolster her courage, as well.

What she was about to say would prompt one of two reactions, both fitting clichés. Either Beck was going to laugh out loud, thinking she'd completely flipped her lid, or he'd grasp the golden opportunity she was about to present to him.

She chewed slowly and swallowed, then she put the biscuit down. She whisked the crumbs off her hands and linked her fingers in her lap. "Elena has instructed me, very specifically, as to what I am to say to you. Please, don't interrupt until I'm through."

A lifted brow was his only reaction.

She looked down at her clasped fingers and realized that she was communicating her tension. "This is difficult for me because I can't be specific. Not because I don't want to explain in detail," she assured him hastily, "but because I can't."

"Go on."

His husky words brought her mind back to her objective. "Yes, well…" She spread her hands, indicating her flimsy resolve. "Seventeen years is a long time. I don't know how much you remember about your grandmother's disposition but she never, *never,* lets anything upset her. Her serenity is legend."

Beck nodded. His expression softened, but he didn't smile. "I remember."

"Elena has been very distressed over the last few months. Her mood has been almost like a shadow hanging over the community. It was clear to everyone around her that something was on her mind, something that disturbed her greatly. When I asked her about it, she said there was nothing I could do for now.

"Then three days ago she called me in and said the time had come for me to help. I was given instructions that sound vague, even to me, and I'm accustomed to vague instructions." She stopped to take a deep breath and crossed one arm across her waist; the other hand went to the necklace. "Elena said that if you had a strong reason for not returning to the community, I was to ascertain if this reason was legitimate. Then I was to tell you that the birthday party was only an excuse. Elena knew—" she gripped the necklace tightly "—somehow, that you were faced with a grave problem relating to your position with the president, one which may seem unsolvable. She wants you to know... She wanted me to tell you that she can help you solve it."

Beck was silent as though waiting for her to give him more information.

She held her hands out, palms up. "That's all she told me. I'm sorry."

"So, I have to go to Shared Ground to find out what her miraculous solution is?"

"Yes," she answered quietly.

He shook his head. "Damn. I can't believe the woman. It's another ploy, Cat. She's using it to get me home. Just like she used you. Well, I'm afraid this problem is unsolvable, even for Elena," he said impatiently. "I wonder how she knew," he added almost as an afterthought.

Catriona took another long, restorative breath. The sound drew his gaze. "Through the years Elena has regularly astonished, astounded and amazed me. She has a great capacity for reflection. She can see sides to a dilemma and depths of solution that I never thought of until she pointed them out. Then they seem so logical, I wonder why I didn't think of them. Still, I don't understand where she gets her information," she said wryly.

He shot her a cynical look. "You haven't talked to her since you got here?"

Catriona rolled her eyes. "I should have expected that, I suppose. She doesn't have a phone." She paused and then continued as though she were swearing in court. "No, Beck, I have not talked to your grandmother or to anyone else in Shared Ground since I arrived in Washington."

"Well, she certainly didn't find out from ABC or CBS," he told her sardonically. "There hasn't been a suggestion of a news leak."

She shook her head helplessly. "I thought maybe you had a hunch."

"Me? I know Elena has her spies, but for the life of me I can't figure out how anyone could have found out. And I refuse to believe in ESP, Cat."

After a minute, she spoke again. "Beck, what if she *could* help the president? Maybe she has prepared something from the garden.... She usually leaves that work to me, but lately she's been working like a demon in the small laboratory she has at home."

When he reacted with a raised brow and a half smile, she realized what she had said. She gave a deprecating chuckle. "You're right. The devil isn't a fitting comparison for Elena. But, Beck, can you afford to refuse?"

He sobered. The tired, drawn look returned to his face. Leaning forward, he propped his elbows on his thighs; his hands dangled between his knees. "Cat, do you honestly think a homemade 'simple' from a primitive physic garden in Tennessee is going to cure the president when the greatest doctors in the world have tried and failed?'' Under the obvious force of genuine despair, his sarcastic demeanor had faded.

"I believe in science, Beck," she said evenly. "Nothing I've learned about the garden is mystical or primitive. I don't deny that she knows more than I do, but I will tell you this. Before synthetic chemicals began to dominate medicine, eighty percent of all drugs were derived from plant materials. The possibilities for discovering new cures have been neglected for many years, but there are scientists that are taking notice.

"Look at what's going on in the Amazon. Scores of people are down there right now, cataloging the plants, trying to save what they can from the disappearing rain forests, because they're afraid the world will lose something invaluable. Even today, one-fourth of all medicines are made from plants, the one-fourth that scientists haven't been able to duplicate in the laboratory. Look at the widespread use of cortisone and its derivatives, look at the birth-control pill. All these drugs are available now as synthetics, but only because of the discovery of a saponin in a lowly Mexican yam."

Beck couldn't resist a smile. She was certainly enthusiastic about her field. Then he sobered. "This is the president, Cat. How can I suggest to him that my grandmother can cure him, when the other experts, medical and scientific, have been stumped?"

"I don't know how you would suggest it to him. At one time I would have doubted right along with you." She rose and began to pace. "But I really don't think you can ignore the possibilities, Beck." She stopped and swung on him. "I do know that I've seen things I can't explain." She came to a stop in front of him, plunging her fists into the pockets of her jacket. She frowned.

"But I'm just the messenger here. Are you willing to take a chance that it couldn't work?"

He sighed.

"My knowledge as Gardener is incomplete. I know that," she said as though she were speaking to herself. "There seems to be a sort of—" she lifted her hand and let it drop "—secret within the confidentiality of Shared Ground. I don't know what it is. Elena has always reserved something, some knowledge. There are plants within the physic garden— I know their individual properties, but she works with them collectively. Yet she refuses to explain other than to give her stock answer, to say that when the time comes, she'll tell me what to do with them. This might be the time, Beck."

She came back to the bench and sat down beside him, leaning forward in her excitement. In spite of his resolve he felt himself responding to her drive, her energy. He made himself concentrate on what she was saying.

"I'm confident that there's nothing mystical about the garden, just a miracle that the modern world hasn't discovered—or maybe *re*discovered—yet."

Beck was surprised to find that, under the influence of Cat's indubitable passion for her subject, he was actually beginning to consider the possibilities.

At the least, he could return to Shared Ground with her, see if there was anything promising there. Today was Friday. If they left Washington right away, they could be at Shared Ground by dinnertime. He could spend tomorrow with his grandmother and come back Sunday.

Good God, what was he thinking of? He stood suddenly and jammed his hands into his trousers' pockets. He jingled the change there, touched the distinctive surface of the medallion. Besides the medical profession, what the hell would the Secret Service have to say if he walked in with an untried, untested medicine to administer to the president?

He almost laughed out loud. What would he say to his boss— Mr. President, here is a little something for you. I'm not sure what is is, but my grandmother swears it will cure your condition?

Besides, there were the negotiations to consider. If they were to salvage anything, he would have to work night and day. He couldn't leave Washington. Not now. It was impossible.

He turned back to Cat. She was watching him expectantly. A breeze lifted a strand of her hair from her chignon and the sunlight shone through. With a tender smile, he reached out to tuck the strand behind her ear. His fingers lingered against the skin on her neck, and he bent forward to brush her lips lightly with his. His hand slid around her nape, tightening there. He kissed her again, harder.

When he finally lifted his head, his husky voice held a trace of real regret. "You can tell my grandmother that she chose the right envoy to push me to the brink," he said gently. "But not quite over the edge, Cat. I can't go with you."

She shook her head to dislodge his touch. She blinked, fighting the sting of tears in her eyes, telling herself they weren't there because of the bittersweet kiss but because she'd failed Elena.

Her fingers curled into her palms. She'd tried, she'd really tried. She would have to go home empty-handed. Elena would look at her, without disapproval but with the poignant smile that was her response to disappointment. "Can't or won't?" she demanded shakily, just as she had last night.

Beck started to give the same answer, when a call from his driver halted his words. Danny stood beside the open door of the limo, the telephone receiver in his hand.

"It's urgent," he called.

Beck's hand was on her shoulder. At the word "urgent" his fingers dug unconsciously into her flesh. "Stay here," he ordered. He ran to the car.

Catriona's heart was in her throat as she watched him take the receiver, listen briefly then hand the phone back to the driver. When he turned back she saw that the blood had drained from his face, leaving him white.

She caught her breath; fear spurred her to move quickly. She hurried to meet him on the path and reached for his hand.

His cold fingers tightened around hers. "The president has collapsed," he said heavily. "I have to go."

"The hospital?"

"No. Evidently he's conscious and alert enough to give specific orders. He feels very strongly—" Beck broke off. "He doesn't want the media to get hold of this until he can make an announcement himself."

Last night she'd seen Beck's anxiety, his frustration, his sense of helplessness over the health of his boss. She'd been a witness to his dismay. This was much worse.

Like a Thoroughbred at the starting gate, he was anxious to be off. Yet he hesitated, looking down at their clasped hands. Then he took a long, deep breath. He seemed to hold it forever before he exhaled. "Go back inside and wait for me. If I don't call before noon, I'll pick you up in front of the hotel then."

She glanced back over her shoulder at his driver, who had the door open and waiting. She realized he'd reached a decision, reluctantly, but he'd reached one. "Are you going back with me?"

"No. Yes." He ran his fingers through his hair. "Hell, I don't know yet. I'm going to see if I can talk to the president."

He was already moving away from her. "Shall I make airline reservations?" she said across the space that separated them.

He glanced back and shook his head. "No. If I decide to go, we'll drive."

As she watched, he climbed into the limousine. The door had barely closed when the vehicle pulled into the traffic and shot off down the street.

Beck was going home to Shared Ground, Catriona realized suddenly. He was going to Tennessee with her. She hadn't failed at her quest after all. She wasn't grateful for the president's deteriorating condition, but she faced the truth. Her arguments, as he had admitted, pushed him right up to the fine edge of acquiescence.

But it had take the president's collapse to push him over.

The White House was only a few blocks away and Danny drove like a rocket. Still the trip seemed to take forever.

Beck sat braced against the seat, impatient and anxious, tension in every muscle of his body. His hand was wrapped around the door handle; he was ready to jump out the minute they reached their destination.

The argument going on inside his head was chaotic and equally as tense as his muscles.

Do I take the chance? he asked himself. *Do I believe in the possibility that Elena can help the president?*

And the counterquestions: *Do I dare not try? What if there's a prospect for the president's recovery and I don't take it? Could I live with myself?*

There would be no personal danger to the president, Beck knew that as surely as he knew his name. Though the Food and Drug Administration would hardly agree with him, and though he'd had his problems with his grandmother and the community she dominated like an ancient overlord, he knew she would never do anything that could conceivably harm anyone.

Elena had the required education and training for her position. Just as his father had been trained, just as his great-grandfather had been, just as he would have been had he chosen to stay and take over the position of Gardener, Elena was a member of a proud band. She would never have sent the message had she not known exactly what she was doing.

Because, as weird as Shared Ground was, the community standards had always been firmly based on honesty, integrity and honor.

Beck was standing at a window in the family quarters, staring out over the vast lawn, seeing nothing. He turned when the president's physician entered the room behind him.

"The president would like to see you now, Beck." Hal's suit seemed two sizes too big and his long, narrow face was seamed with worry.

"How is he?"

Hal shook his head. "Worse than last night, probably better than tomorrow."

Beck nodded and followed the man down the hall to the bedroom. When he entered, he was shocked by the pallor of the man on the bed. Fighting to speak past a lump in his throat, he crossed the room to stand beside his boss. "How are you feeling?"

"Like I've been run over by a tank," said the man weakly. "But I'll survive."

Beck had been witness to many of the president's weak spells over the past few months, but this one was worse than anything he'd ever seen before. There was a vulnerability to him so unlike his normal demeanor that Beck had to school his expression to hide his alarm.

The president went on, "Beck, I wouldn't admit this to another living soul." The bleak eyes took on a further grief and Beck knew to whom the man referred.

The president's late wife, the beautiful woman who had been the victim of a terrorist bomb and to whose memory he had dedicated the negotiations, had been his friend and closest confidante.

"I've reached the end of my endurance. God only knows what will happen to the negotiations, but unless you can come up with another idea, I'm going to have to resign immediately."

Me? thought Beck. It was an odd suggestion coming from this man.

The president was looking at him hopefully. "Beck, is there anything we haven't tried?"

Suddenly he was struck with a thought. In their years together, they had often talked of their families. The president knew that Beck's parents were dead, that his grandmother was the titular head of a clan of spiritualistic Scots, guardians of a remote physic garden. Could he possibly...?

No. Impossible.

"Anything at all?" the president demanded, his voice suddenly vibrant.

For an instant Beck had a glimpse of the spirit he'd always admired so much. It was there in the older man's eyes, a combination of will and indignation, a hint of the old aggressive energy that seemed to have endured beyond any natural expectation.

The glimpse was fleeting, like a photographer's flash... and just as quickly extinguished.

Beck avoided that steady gaze. Hell. The president was looking to him to do something, but this wasn't a campaign glitch that could be handled with a phone call. This wasn't a world crisis that couldn't be handled at all, but simply had to be waded through. And he certainly wasn't a miracle worker.

He yearned for his leader, his mentor, not this weakened man struck down so cruelly by an ephemeral, unknown enemy, one that couldn't be fought, because it wouldn't reveal itself. It was like boxing in earnest with a shadow. What did the president expect of him? And yet, the coincidence, the timing, could it be that Elena had somehow sensed...?

Beck cleared his throat. "Mr. President, I'm not sure what you're asking of me," he began quietly. "But we have ten days before the negotiating team meets again. May I suggest that you go to Camp David for the weekend, to rest," he said, mentioning the presidential retreat. "The press won't question the announcement—not with the schedule you've been keeping lately."

His expression took on a determined cast. "And, while you're resting, I'd like permission to return to my grandmother's home in Tennessee for the weekend."

The president looked at him, briefly disconcerted, but, Beck noted, not particularly surprised by the unexpected request. Not even as surprised as Beck himself was.

He wondered when he'd made his decision to return to Shared Ground. He supposed he'd known from the minute he saw Cat that this was what it would come down to.

No matter how long or how far he ran, he'd always known that he couldn't completely escape the community. A part of Shared Ground would always be there, like another arm, because that part was within him.

He couldn't explain the magnet that drew him, not even to himself. He was going back; he was going to question his grandmother. If there was magic to be found within Shared Ground, he'd use it—he'd use anything it took—to restore this man to vibrant health.

Keen eyes searched Beck's expression; their gazes met and held. They communicated on another level of consciousness, the young dedicated man and his diminished mentor, a level of perception rare between human beings, a level founded on trust, in themselves, in each other.

This meeting of the minds was nothing new to either of them; they'd always had this empathy. Some said they were on the same wavelength, had been since the young Beck MacDomhall had walked into the Missouri congressman's campaign headquarters.

"Your grandmother is quite elderly if I remember correctly," said the president.

"Yes, sir, she will soon celebrate her one hundredth birthday."

"Then of course you must go."

"Thank you, sir. I'll leave right away. When I get back Sunday, I'll come directly to Camp David in time to return to Washington with you. I..." He let his voice trail off.

He'd been going to say that he hoped he'd have—if not a solution, then at least an expectation of one. But he couldn't let the president believe he'd come back to Washington with a miracle cure, when he didn't know himself if he'd find one.

Chapter 4

Beck pulled through the circular driveway in front of the Arrowhead Hotel at three-thirty. It had begun to rain again and he was about to turn the car over to the parking attendant when he spotted Catriona.

Evidently she had been watching the driveway. She raised her hand and came through the doors, carrying a small suitcase. He watched between the intermittent sweep of the wipers as the uniformed doorman took the case from her and opened his umbrella over her head while they descended the broad sweep of steps together. She said something to him and smiled. The man's answering smile wavered with signs of conundrum.

Beck could certainly understand the doorman's reaction—her smile confused the hell out of him, too.

Even as a child, Cat could always accomplish anything with that smile. So when Beck had wanted a treat or permission, he would send her to ask his mother, his father or Elena. And she went willingly.

To Catriona, whatever Beck wanted, Beck should have. In those days he'd been her hero. He'd treated her casually; she was a cute kid. But deep down he'd liked being somebody's hero.

When his father, John, had finally figured out what was going on, he had reacted angrily—a rare occurrence, to see John MacDomhall angry. He'd told Beck that he mustn't treat Catriona like his own personal servant.

When he had bolted Shared Ground for good, he'd effectively killed the hero worship. For a moment Beck felt the unhappy weight of regret; he should not have left without at least saying goodbye to her. But he'd had unbearable grief and agony to deal with. The emotions had retreated over the intervening years into a lonely corner of his mind, but they'd never faded completely.

He chuckled to himself, a dry, unamused sound as the doorman said something and she flashed the smile again. Her indisputable poise was apparent to any observer, but this afternoon her demeanor seemed to be lightly spiced with a quaint, otherworldly cast. Yesterday, she'd acted nervous; today she was totally assured. It wasn't hard to figure out. She was going home.

Aside from her startling beauty, she was really no different from any of a dozen other women who entered and left the area. Her clothes were casual. She had changed into slacks, a loose cotton sweater and flat-heeled canvas shoes for the trip. A raincoat was slung over her shoulders. Her hair, in one long, fat braid, spilled forward over her shoulder. Today her serenity seemed as firmly fixed as Elena's.

They reached the bottom of the steps. Ignoring the pouring rain, Beck got out of the car, took her suitcase from the doorman and stowed it in the trunk of his small black convertible, getting thoroughly wet in the process.

The man opened the passenger door and helped Cat in, made sure the edges of her raincoat were tucked out of the way and touched the brim of his hat, all as respectfully and carefully as if she were visiting royalty.

Beck dug into his pocket and pulled out a bill. When he joined her on the front seat he was soaked, but she barely had a hair out of place. He reached behind him for a towel he kept in the back. He offered the towel to her, but she shook her head. He dried his face and hair. "Sorry I'm late," he muttered.

She pulled the strap of the seat belt over her shoulder and clicked it into place. "That's okay. We can still get home before Elena goes to bed."

Her words stopped him, then he sighed and threw the towel into the back seat. He combed the damp strands away from his face. "Look, Cat, let's get something straight right from the start. I'm not going home, you are. I'm escorting you because I don't seem to have a choice. But I will not stay at Shared Ground for any longer than it takes to do what I have to do." He broke off. "What are you smiling about?"

She turned her gaze on him; the smile faded. He was struck by her expression of melancholy. He slipped the car into gear but kept his foot on the brake, letting himself be beguiled for a moment by her beautiful green eyes while he waited for her to answer.

"I'm smiling because, ironically, those are the exact words I used myself when I arrived in Washington," she explained softly.

"Cat, Washington is my home," he finally said, feeling that somehow he was losing control again.

"Yes, I know."

Dragging his gaze away from hers, he clenched his teeth and took his foot off the brake.

"I can help you drive, if you like."

"No, thanks," he declared, his tone laced with inflexibility. "I don't like to be driven."

"Then why—"

"The president's idea," he said shortly. "This is my car."

"I like it."

At that, he relented, smiled even. Obviously he loved his small sports car.

Catriona was beginning to understand Beck a bit better. He wouldn't want to surrender control to anyone. She watched his strong, competent hands on the wheel. He did mindless things like that with such grace, such assurance, as though he considered the workings of his muscles to be a piece of machinery, as though he'd trained his body to respond in a certain way and didn't entertain the slightest doubt that it would respond accordingly.

There was nothing tentative about this man, not one thing; and, she speculated, there was endurance in him that hadn't even been tapped yet. He was very masculine in his confidence.

She felt heat rising in her blood as she remembered last night's kiss, so powerful, so all-encompassing. And the briefer version this morning.

She wondered if she would ever know another kiss like his, would ever know another man like him. The idea that she might not saddened her immensely.

Beck pulled out into the heavy Friday-afternoon traffic of the nation's capital. The engine of the small car gave a lusty roar.

She felt as though they were beginning a long trip to another kind of land altogether, a place of the past, remote and isolated in the Tennessee mountains. But, though he didn't know it, a place as modern as tomorrow.

Beck was a fast driver but a good one. They stopped once for gasoline and once in southwestern Virginia for a quick hamburger. When they were on the road again, Catriona glanced across the seat, trying to judge his mood before she spoke.

He could be left to discover most of the changes in Shared Ground for himself. But she needed to explain a few of the things he was about to see before they arrived.

"I should warn you that you won't be able to drive all the way into the valley. You'll have to park your car on the mountain."

Caught unaware, he turned to stare at her. He quickly returned his eyes to the road, but clearly she had startled him. She held back a grin.

"Why? And how the hell do we get there?" he asked. "If I recall, the village is not exactly accessible on foot."

"First questions first," she said lightly. Not waiting for him to answer, she went on, "We've banned internal combustion engines."

"You've what?"

She looked over at him. "The story goes way back. Perhaps I'd better start at the beginning so you'll understand better," she said, her voice rising as if it were a question.

"Other than along this road, I can't see that we're going anywhere."

She turned sideways in her seat and tucked one foot under her. "After your parents were killed and Elena had to resume her duties—" she paused but he didn't react visibly "—she realized quickly that if the community were to prosper, there would have to be some changes. The Garden was the center of the community, but she decided to encourage technological development, as well. Mostly on an experimental scale.

"Years ago—" she frowned, trying to recall "—about ten or twelve years, if I remember correctly, the children in the community started to get these awful coughs. We had cough remedies, of course, and they'd always been effective, but they didn't help this time. We also began to have trouble with some of the plants, some of the rarer ones that have always been tough to keep alive. They began to deteriorate. The doctors—"

"Doctors?" Beck interrupted. "You have real doctors in Shared Ground?"

"I told you, we've been recruiting new people into Shared Ground for more than fifteen years now," she answered testily. "Of course we have doctors."

The conversation was getting interesting, thought Beck. He remembered as a child having to travel twenty-two miles to the county seat to have a broken bone set. Of course, Shared Ground wasn't the only rural community that didn't have medical care available. "Trained at Johns Hopkins, I presume," he teased, but with a strong dose of skepticism.

Catriona smiled to herself. He really was in for a big surprise. "I told you there have been many changes in Shared Ground." She paused for effect. "But not Johns Hopkins. Duke. At least one of them is. Shall I continue?"

"Get on with it," he muttered.

"The doctors did some investigating and discovered that the problem was air pollution, something we'd never been bothered by until the community started to grow."

"Just how big is the community?" The population was about eight hundred when he left.

"We try to keep it at around fifteen hundred. For the available space and water, you see. We are careful not to outstrip our natural resources. We're working on ways to..." Her voice trailed off, and she waved a hand to indicate that she was digressing from the subject. "Excuse me. I tend to get on my soapbox. Anyway, the doctors recommended that we do away with all the engines. So we did. Within a month the children's coughs cleared up completely."

"Good God," he breathed, his interest aroused in spite of his determination to remain detached. "How the hell did you do that?" He had a mental picture in his mind of them hauling everything in and out by mule and wagon.

"We're determined to rely only on natural energy sources. Our engineers—" She hesitated, waiting for him to make another scornful remark like the one about the doctors.

Engineers? Seventeen years ago Beck had left a community dominated by impractical philosophers and innocents. Now it seemed he was returning to a community with more than a few pragmatists. He wondered what other changes he would find.

Farmers and shopkeepers, farriers and teachers, they had always led a simple life but one rich in pride and tradition. They worked hard, but there were diversions, as well. He remembered summertime: the weekly concerts in the garden, the cookouts, the pickup ball games.

He remembered winter: the impromptu bonfires, ice skating on the pond—when the pond ice was frozen solidly enough—the plays performed in the elementary school auditorium.

In contrast he thought of his friends in Washington and how they worried about their children. But worry was about all they had the time for with both parents working to make ends meet. As a result the children were often unruly, willful and unhappy. Childhood was so organized nowadays that seldom was an activity enjoyed for the pure fun of it.

Those observations were the prime reasons he'd avoided marriage and fatherhood. If he couldn't give a family more than his leftover time, he wouldn't have one.

He realized that her pause had stretched into an extended silence, an invitation for him to comment on her last remark. But Beck wasn't about to touch that one. "Go on," he said evenly.

He listened more closely as Cat resumed her explanation. "Our engineers developed and constructed a new kind of power plant. They've harnessed natural sources of energy, the wind, the sun and water on a large scale. And, best of all, they've discovered ways to store all the power we need for a long, long time. I don't pretend to understand how it works, but it does work."

Beck felt his excitement build as his mind began to leap over the possibilities. "How, in God's name...?" he said to himself. If the engineers in Shared Ground had really figured out ways to store energy efficiently and for long periods, the potential for the rest of the country was staggering.

"I keep up with the current experimental work on alternative energy sources," he said carefully. "But I haven't heard of any new developments reaching the production stage."

Catriona gnawed at her lower lip. Beck would, in his job capacity, be familiar with such work. She wondered why she hadn't thought of that. "The ideas were experimental, at first. Luckily Elena was quick to recognize that the world was changing and we had to change with it or be swallowed up. One of the attributes we look for when we recruit is a creative, independent spirit, an individual who isn't leashed to yesterday's logic, who isn't afraid to think for him—or her—self." Amusement colored her voice as she continued. "We also try to avoid tying our engineers' hands with administrative red tape."

"Touché," he said softly. He was silent and thoughtful as he absorbed the information. But as his euphoria wore off, he became more cautious. He had hundreds of questions for her but he would wait. He'd have to see for himself how things really worked.

Particularly the recruiting part. How did they convince able people to walk away from civilization and into a backwater community like Shared Ground? "So where do we park the car?" he asked.

"In a cave near the crest of the mountain. We'll take one of our community vehicles into town."

"You have your own vehicles?" That was hard to believe. How did they manufacture vehicles?

"We've modified existing cars and trucks. Don't worry, you won't have to hike in."

"Good."

Catriona yawned. That should be enough information to hold him for now, and her lack of sleep was catching up with her. "If you don't mind I think I'll close my eyes for a bit."

Beck nodded. "Sure," he said absently. He had a lot to think about. So—they recruited new people, did they? So—how did they keep Shared Ground isolated?

He glanced across at her and she gave him a sweet, innocent smile. He'd stop the questions for now. He'd observe instead.

Catriona had fallen asleep. She'd slept through the point where they left the interstate highway; she'd slept on when they left the state highway for the secondary roads that wound through the mountains; but when she felt the first bumps beneath the wheels, she opened her eyes. They had made the first of the twisting turns onto the rough back-country roads that gave Shared Ground its protection from casual visitors.

Beck hit a rut and swore.

Catriona sat up, wriggling around in the seat to relieve the points on her body that had been uncomfortably pressured. "What time is it?" she asked, her voice husky from sleep.

Beck looked over at the clock on the dashboard, surprised that it wasn't later. "It's eleven-twenty."

"We've made good time."

He hit another rut and swore again. "No wonder this place hasn't been discovered by the mountain developers yet. Who would want it?"

She smiled across at him. "As a matter of fact, we had some developers nosing around last year. They had flown over and seen the village from the air. With the help of a state environmental group, we managed to convince them that it wouldn't be economically feasible to develop the property."

The village that he remembered was small, encompassing only about a hundred acres, and divided by two main streets running parallel and three or four that bisected at right angles. But all the available land for miles around had been owned by the villagers, bought up to augment the original land grants and to protect the community from unwanted intrusions. He wondered if they were still buying land.

"Besides, no one in Shared Ground would sell an inch to unwanted outsiders, right?" he declared with grudging admiration. It wasn't often in this day and time that someone couldn't be bought, especially if the price, like that offered by some of the more successful developers, was ridiculously high.

Cat grinned back. "Right." She stretched with her arms out in front of her, bowing her back, linking her fingers and turning them inside out. She let her head fall forward between her arms. "The people of Shared Ground aren't foolish, Beck. They realize that the lifestyle they enjoy can't be bought for any amount of money," she said softly. Without a break she switched subjects. "Oh, I'll be so glad to sleep in my own bed tonight."

Beck doubted that all the people of Shared Ground were so exemplary. But he couldn't think of another explanation for the continued isolation of the community.

He glanced over at her, his expression curious, another question on his lips. Then he wished he hadn't looked at her. Warm with sleep, her vulnerable nape exposed, her sensual appeal was increased. His imagination took the thought a step further. Cat, her beautiful eyes veiled by drowsy lids, her hair spread across a pillow, her body clad only in moonlight...

He shifted uncomfortably in the seat and forced the intriguing picture out of his mind. "Where do you live, Cat? With Elena?"

She turned in the seat to face him. Her enthusiasm was evident; it seemed that the closer to Shared Ground she got, the happier she was. "No. I've had my own place since the year after I graduated from college. It's on the far side of the garden from your grandmother's." The soft laughter curved her tempting lips. "I helped build it myself."

He noted gratefully that there would be six acres separating them. The way he felt right now, he'd need every one of those acres like a barrier to keep them apart.

Despite the grave reasons for this trip, his libido had been strained by her proximity during the long drive. She was unconsciously sexy and feminine. Being alone with her for hours in this tiny confined space, being subjected to the delicate scent of her perfume, the cadence of her musical voice and worse, the soft, sexy sighs that emerged from her lips as she slept, had sorely stretched his self-control.

He hit a pothole. "Damn." Suddenly he was faced with a fork in the road, one he didn't seem to remember. "Which way?" he asked.

She gave him an odd look. "To the right."

"It's been a while," he excused himself.

She looked down at her folded hands. "Yes, it has," she said.

For the first time, he realized just how long it had been. When he left he'd been a youngster. He was separated from this place not only by distance, but by time, outlook and experience.

What was he going to say to his grandmother? Unobtrusively he rubbed his hand on his jeans-covered thigh.

He felt for a moment like a kid who's about to face punishment for a serious infraction of parental rules.

"She will be so happy to see you that she won't say a word about how long it's been."

He grinned ruefully. "How did you know what I was thinking? Maybe you've learned more from Elena than you'll admit to."

She raised an arched brow, distracting him again. "Your thoughts weren't very hard to read. We're almost there."

Because of the rough going, he'd slowed the car to a crawl and he was barely moving when Cat suddenly said, "Turn here."

It seemed the community had utilized one of the many caves that dotted these mountains as the equivalent to a parking garage. Following Cat's directions he found the entrance, which was effectively disguised with native plants and not detectable from the road.

He steered the car through an opening, probably twenty feet high and fifteen feet wide. As soon as the entrance was breached, the sound of the engine grew louder, amplified by the enclosed space. The headlights picked out crags in the irregular granite walls.

He parked in the spot Cat indicated and switched off the engine. Darkness and silence suddenly fell upon them like a cloak. The only noise was that of the heated engine, which gave a snap as it began to cool. And there was no light at all.

The huge dark cavern gave Beck the feeling of being entombed and he didn't like it. He gave a half-serious thought to turning the car around and getting the hell out of there. But he couldn't do that. Like Cat he had made a journey to fulfill a mission; and, like her, he'd be damned if he wouldn't carry it out.

And then he began to be aware of something else—not a light, but a decrease of the darkness. Contours took shape. He stared through the windshield, studying the irregular walls of the cave. The illumination had to be coming from somewhere but he couldn't locate a source.

Like a flash, Cat was out of the car and stretching, her hands at the small of her back. "Oh, its good to move," she said, her delight almost tangible now that she was close to home. "Come on."

"Where's the light coming from?" he asked, opening his door. He had his answer immediately. Where the floor met the walls he saw an edging, like a thin rope, that glowed. "Who switched it on?"

Cat laughed. "You did, as you drove through the entrance. The system works like one of those burglar alarms that responds to heat and movement. We have the same kind of system in our homes, too. Saves a lot of energy in case you forget to turn off the lights when you leave a room."

He smiled wryly to himself as he locked the doors of the car, ignoring her pointed look, then he opened the trunk to remove their luggage.

She led the way to a group of three vehicles. Beck eyed them warily. Two of them looked like stripped-down dune buggies or expanded golf carts. The third had once been a truck. She indicated one of the smaller vehicles. He slung the two cases into the back and started to get in under the wheel.

"Maybe I should drive," she suggested politely. "Just until you're familiar with the system."

His jaw clamped down. But he slid across the seat without comment. To his surprise Cat slid the gold chain with its charm over her head. She slipped the disk into a slot on the dash that he hadn't noticed before. All at once, there was a hum from beneath the hood.

"What the hell...?"

"You'll see," she said again. And they were off. "Do you know the history of the stone shavings in our disks?"

He searched his memory. "I don't think...wait a minute. Wasn't there a myth? The stone in the north corner of the garden was brought with the first settlers from Scotland. No one was ever quite sure why." He could picture the stone, remembered it being about the size of a television set.

"Yes. Even in the logs, the references were always vague as to the stone's importance."

Beck had forgotten about the log, a huge ledgerlike book—actually a series of books—in his father's, no Elena's, study. Each year the Gardener entered all the important things that had happened since the last entry. Records of births and deaths, crop yields, trading arrangements, new cultures from the garden.

"Elena worked with the two engineers who were recruited first. She said that she'd always felt there had to be a use for the odd stone. It took several years but finally they found it. Some property in the stone reacts to magnets and activates the energy source that runs the cars. She thinks there may be other things the stone will do, as well."

Beck was speechless. He also wondered if he was losing his mind, or had stepped through the looking glass.

Moments later, Cat maneuvered the vehicle around a curve and there it was, spread out in the valley before them. Without being asked, she stopped to give him time to look.

The moonlight painted the lush summer landscape in silver and white. Beck had been to Scotland a few years ago. But only now did he realize how similar Shared Ground was to the villages he'd visited there. Spellbound, he stared at the town, swallowing suddenly over a lump that had formed in his throat.

Home.

No. He fought against that concept, against the feelings that suddenly seized him. Shared Ground *was* no longer his home.

And yet there was something he couldn't deny, something that tugged at him ... here lay the origin of his spirit, his source. Desperately he tried to shake off the emotions, but his vision was unexpectedly blurred. His glasses, why hadn't he had them checked? Hell, he was no sentimental fool. He wouldn't allow this place to get a grip on him. He couldn't.

With a tremendous effort, he forced himself to ignore the blurred vision, to look dispassionately at the scene before him. It was a small town, like thousands of other small towns across the country. No more, no less.

Seen from this height, the same structures he remembered lined the miniature streets. The buildings were substantial, their rock facades mined from the mountains by his ancestors over two hundred years ago. The outward appearance had not changed, he thought at first. Then he corrected the thought.

The town below him was larger, more densely packed than he remembered. Farther from the hub of the crossroads, the buildings were still spread out, sitting within the borders of neatly trimmed shrubbery on manicured lawns. But there were more of them.

At last, as though he had been postponing the most difficult part of this whole journey, his gaze slid lightly across the heart of Shared Ground, searching for the garden, and then touching down gingerly. It was as if he were testing a wound for tenderness, afraid to settle his gaze too firmly on the spot where his parents were buried. There.

He inhaled deeply, filling his lungs. His father—so strong, so brilliant, so loving. His mother—so beautiful, so generous, so caring.

He searched further, looking for the Gardener's house, where he'd grown up, where he and his parents and Elena had lived for the first seventeen years of his life.

He exhaled slowly. The house—so unbearably empty when they died.

Despite Elena's presence. Despite the community's concern, despite everything, he'd fled. Not from responsibility. From the emptiness.

He stared for a long minute at the lonely light in Elena's window. He supposed that, in her way, his grandmother attempted to be amiable, but he'd never felt close to her. His father, her son, was Elena's shining star.

Cat had been silent while he took his visual inventory. He spoke then, but his gaze didn't veer from the scene below. "Help me, Cat," he appealed hoarsely. "I can't let Elena get the idea that I'm home to stay. I don't want to hurt her."

Anyone who knew Beck MacDomhall would have been stunned by such signs of uncertainty and self-doubt. To tell the truth he was surprised himself.

On impulse Catriona reached for his hand. She linked her fingers with his. "I'm glad you're concerned for Elena. She would like to think you'd stay forever, but she harbors no illusion on that score, Beck, I promise.

Neither will anyone else. We'll just be glad to have you with us, for however long you are able to stay."

He turned to her, lifted a brow. "Even you?"

"Even me." She tilted her head. Her smile became a grin, but he could see that she was also emotionally touched. "Particularly me. I want to be the Gardener officially, remember?"

He tightened his grip on her hand, raised it to his mouth. Over their clasped fingers, their eyes met and held. Her skin was like velvet; he moved his lips across her knuckles. His heart took comfort from the affinity he felt emanating from her, like a field of energy. It was both a momentary solace and, at the same time, scary as hell. "Thanks, Cat."

He reluctantly let go of her hand; she eased the vehicle forward and started to descend the mountain.

Chapter 5

Shock catapulted Beck from the chair where he'd been sitting and across the room to his grandmother's side. "A year? You want me to stay here for an entire year in exchange for this potion you say is some kind of miracle cure?"

"A year of your time is a small price to pay," his grandmother said adamantly. She met his angry gaze without flinching, and he tried to breathe deeply, to restore the pleasant calm he'd felt when they'd arrived.

He and Catriona had come directly to Elena's cottage. They had arrived less than an hour ago. Elena's greeting had been matter-of-fact. They'd eaten the meal she had waiting for them, mostly in silence, which Elena seemed to excuse on the basis of their long trip, and returned to the formal parlor. That was when she'd dropped her bomb.

Beck had been surprised to see that much of the house was exactly as it had been seventeen years ago. A few pieces of furniture had been reupholstered and the kitchen had been remodeled, but his father's desk—Elena's desk now—still sat before the window of the study and his mother's delicate watercolors still hung above the breakfront in the dining room.

Elena's small, erect figure looked lost in the large wing chair. With unwelcome nostalgia, he remembered his father filling it easily. He cut the thought off.

Dressed in a simple cotton housedress the color of asters, the familiar medallion on a delicate chain around her neck, Elena held her chin high, with the impeccable bearing that was so much a part of her. Elena never forgot who she was.

Her hair was short, neatly coiffed in a turn of white curls and her cornflower-blue eyes were only slightly faded by age. She might be ninety-nine, but she certainly didn't look that old.

But she was just as combative as he'd remembered.

Now, fists planted firmly on his hips, he stared down at her in disbelief.

He scowled. "There's no way I can leave my job for a year." He turned his angry gaze to Catriona. "Did you know this was going to be a condition when you came to Washington?" he demanded.

Cat's lips were colorless. She opened her mouth, but before she could speak, Elena answered for her. "Catriona did not even know of the existence of the compound. I only decided on the condition myself last night," she said smoothly. After generations in America, her voice still retained the slight Scottish burr of her forefathers. He'd forgotten how soft and pleasing it was to the ear.

Frustrated, Beck raked a hand through his hair and swung away to stare out the window. "I don't even know if this damned witch's brew will be effective," he muttered.

"I do not appreciate your sarcasm, Beck," she said regally. "You should show some respect for the accomplishments of your ancestors," she went on serenely. "The recipe for this blend of alkaloids has been handed down through many generations. It has rarely been used, and then only for exceptional persons, persons who, in their scope of history, were absolutely vital to the survival of good in the world."

Beck swung back to pin her with his angry gaze. "And who sits in judgment?" he demanded in a dangerously low voice. "Who decides which human being is more deserving of the compound than another?"

Cat moved as though to interrupt, but he halted her with a sharp gesture. "Who makes this choice? Who plays God, Elena?" he continued on relentlessly, though he knew the answer.

For the first time since they'd entered the room, Elena's imperious expression seemed to slip. She turned pale and looked aside, avoiding his determined gaze. "The Gardener decides," she answered, her voice faltering.

"Having the power to make that decision would be an appalling burden," mused Beck, an ominous thought taking shape in his mind.

"The most terrible responsibility you can imagine," agreed Elena. "Especially terrible because of its rarity. It can only be readied every second generation."

"Where did this potion come from?" he demanded.

She gestured with a blue-veined hand toward the wall where a portrait of John MacDomhall hung, indicating the generations that had preceded them. "I'm afraid the origins are lost somewhere in the mists of time. John

MacDomhall brought the plants and the knowledge of the formula to this country when he emigrated from Scotland. The formula was passed on to me by my father, from his father.''

''And my father? Was it passed on to him?''

''He had just begun his studies, when—'' Her voice broke off.

The long, tense silence that followed was ended when Beck said, ''My father didn't want the responsibility, did he, Elena?''

''None of us wants it.''

Suddenly Beck's features twisted into a mask of grief. ''Did my father kill himself to avoid having to accept such a commitment?'' he asked very softly.

His grandmother recoiled as though she'd been struck.

''Good God, Beck!'' said Catriona. ''Are you crazy?'' She took a step forward but was waved away.

Beck didn't remove his gaze from Elena as he answered. ''Yes, maybe I am.''

Elena met his eyes. They did silent battle. ''I will never know the answer to that question, will I?'' she admitted in a whisper. Then she shifted in her chair, regaining her straight posture, and went on in her normal tone. ''But the formula is absolutely invaluable to humanity. If I didn't believe that, I could not go on. I could quote you some instances which, if you know your world history, would be startling examples of its value. At certain times, for certain people...'' Her voice trailed off. She was quiet for a minute. When she spoke again, her voice had strengthened. ''Mankind has continued to search for a fountain of youth. This compound is infinitely more precious.''

"The president is one of those people?" Beck knew the answer—he knew of the vital talks that were going on—but she didn't.

"Yes, he is. Particularly at this moment in our history." She ignored Beck's startled double take, his narrowed eyes. "But the compound is not something that can be prepared on the spur of the moment. It takes careful cultivation and, in the case of a single ingredient, years to isolate its important properties."

Another thought, one so heinous as to be inconceivable, surfaced in Beck's mind. Could Elena be responsible in some way for the president's illness? The idea was dismissed almost as soon as it formed, but he spoke too quickly. "Then you were certain it would be needed?"

Some sort of strange communication seemed to have kicked in between the two of them. Though his words could have been interpreted in several ways, she read his suspicion exactly. She also comprehended his dismissal of that suspicion.

She turned on him, her blue eyes snapping. "That was unworthy of you, Beck," she accused. She gave him a small smile. "But I understand your doubts and your questions. I'm sure that is only one of many you will have for Catriona and me when you return from Washington."

Ah, yes, he'd have questions. Hundreds of them, for starters. But for now he put them all on hold. "*If* I return," he said.

She ignored that.

Beck took a deep breath and exhaled slowly. The antagonism that had jumped back and forth between them like a bouncing ball suddenly seemed to fade. He raked his fingers through his hair and came back to where she

Shared Ground

was sitting. He went down on one knee beside her chair, searching her expression. "I'm sorry, Elena, for the suggestion of any misdeed. I know you would never do that. But something must have prompted you to get this thing ready at this particular time."

She lowered her head in acknowledgment. The color returned to her cheeks. "I shouldn't have to explain that to you, Beck. If you hadn't left here when you did—" She looked down at her hands folded neatly in her lap.

After a minute, he spoke again. "What if this miracle alkaloid compound doesn't cure the president?"

"If it doesn't, you remain in Washington. You don't take up your work here. It's that simple. But if it does work, I expect you to keep your word."

He took one of her hands. It seemed lost between his big ones. "Elena, that is blackmail," he accused, but not unkindly this time.

He was beginning to mellow toward the old woman. He admired the pride with which she'd met his tactlessness. God help him, he was beginning to believe in her hocus-pocus. He really *was* grasping at straws.

"Of course," she replied, smiling.

"When can I have it?" he asked.

"This minute, if you like. I have prepared the vial for travel." She tilted her head and her smile became tender. "However, I had hoped you might stay the night. You've had a long trip."

Beck glanced at his watch. Despite his impatience to be gone, he realized the folly of driving off without at least a few hours' rest. "You're right. I'll get some sleep before I start out." His gaze swung to Catriona. "I'll take you to your house."

Catriona had stayed out of the line of fire during their exchange, but she was more than just a little annoyed with this man. He'd been far more harsh than the circumstances warranted.

His callous accusation about his father's death and the offensive remark about Elena's possible foreknowledge had roused emotions within her that weren't easy to control. She was shocked at his hostility. Though it was brief, and though Elena seemed to have forgiven him, she certainly felt no inclination to do so.

She held on to her anger but strove to keep her voice and expression under control. "No. It's only a short walk through the garden."

"Your suitcase is in the... What do you call them? Buggies?"

"We call them cars," she said evenly. "I'll get it in the morning."

"I'll get it."

She shrugged. When he was gone, she spoke to Elena. "He's changed a lot," she suggested noncommittally.

"Yes, he has. But he has been taken unaware. He's understandably irritated and confused," answered Elena with a sly grin. "He'll feel the weight of many more surprises when he returns. Swallow your anger, my dear. We'll have to make allowances until he's settled here."

"Allowances?" derided Catriona. "It seems to me he could make a few."

"But he won't. He'll fight us every step of the way. How was your trip?"

Catriona wondered about the smile on Elena's lips as she deliberately switched the subject. "Awful," she answered. "I'm glad to be home." At that moment Beck came back inside carrying her suitcase.

She picked up her raincoat and bent to touch her lips to Elena's cheek. The skin there was paper thin and dry and slightly warm. Automatically she put her fingers to the old woman's forehead. "You're not ill, are you?" she asked.

"Certainly not," said Elena, offended.

Catriona smiled. "I'll see you in the morning then. Good night," she said to both of them, and reached for her case.

He didn't release it. "I'll walk over with you."

She didn't want to spend any more time in his presence tonight. She was tired and she might say something she'd regret. "That isn't necessary," she said quickly. "I know you're tired and you'll want to get an early start tomorrow."

The truth was she didn't want his company. Her anger still simmered. She wanted some time alone under the stars, some time to refresh her feelings, to let the mountain breeze blow away the wretched cobwebs of the city—and a few emotional cobwebs, as well.

Beck didn't bother to answer. His expression was unreadable as he walked to the door that led directly into the garden and opened it. His hand on the knob, he waited for her to precede him.

"Stubborn, too," she muttered under her breath as she gathered up her raincoat and purse.

"I'll be right back," said Beck to his grandmother.

They entered the lush, aromatic garden, their footsteps crisp on the gravel beneath their feet. Catriona was pleased to locate a rush of energy. She moved out in front on the path, walking fast.

Beck watched Cat's haughty chin, her stiff shoulders, her swaying backside, with a small smile. He wondered if she was about to discharge some of that anger in his direction.

Sure enough.

"What the *hell* did you think you were doing back there?" she flung at him as soon as they were out of earshot.

"Calm down."

"Calm down? You were insulting, do you know that?"

"I know that Elena and I understand each other," he said firmly. "Did you really expect me to take some unknown substance to Washington with me and administer it to the president of the United States without asking any questions? She knew better." He paused. "I have a few questions for you, too."

She glared at him. "Well, you can take my share and—"

"Do you know anything about this formula I'm taking back?"

Catriona bit off what she'd been about to say and crossed her arms beneath her breasts. "No. As I told you in Washington, I've always suspected there was something special about the garden. But this is the first I've heard Elena speak specifically of the formula. I had hoped..." She left the sentence unfinished.

"You had hoped she would eventually share the secret with you?"

She nodded. "Yes," she admitted quietly. Her anger died away, leaving deep disappointment. "I suppose I had hoped she trusted me enough."

He caught her elbow and stopped her in the middle of the path. His expression was grim. "Cat, it isn't that she doesn't trust you, don't you see? Elena is an anachronism. Tradition dictates her decision, not trust. Even if I have to stay for the year I pledged, I will leave eventually. You'll be her heir apparent again. Nothing will change." He dropped his hand. "Do you believe me?"

After a minute, she nodded. The soft breeze had cooled her anger somewhat. But his statement had also prompted other, more familiar, emotions. Rejection and abandonment, which of course was ridiculous. "Yes, I believe you," she said finally.

She had been telling the truth when she said that his presence here, for however long, would be appreciated by the entire community. But he was mistaken when he said things would be the same after he left. She turned and proceeded along the path again, past the sweet vernal grass, the berry thickets.

"Cat. Catriona." She slowed at the sound of her given name. He rarely called her Catriona.

He was beside her. "Don't walk away from me," he commanded grimly.

"I beg your pardon?" she said, tensing at the arrogant self-confidence in the order. Her chin rose, even though she was fully aware that her rumpled appearance must hamper her own authority. She probably looked like an urchin. "Maybe you're a bit too accustomed to having your orders followed?"

His mouth quirked at one corner. "Sorry," he said, but he didn't look sorry.

He trailed his thumb across her colorless lips, provoking a shiver of sensual awareness. "Beck, we've both had a long day."

She was unaware of the lovely picture she presented, her face washed in moonlight. But her beautiful cat's eyes were troubled, thought Beck. "What is it?" he asked, letting his eyes roam over her lips. He dropped her suitcase on the ground and took her other shoulder in his hand.

She offered no resistance as he brought her closer. She wanted his mouth on hers, wanted it with a yearning she hadn't experienced before.

She closed her eyes.

He bent his head.

But at the last moment she turned her face away. His lips brushed her cheek. "Beck, don't. Please," she whispered.

His fingers tightened for an instant, then he dropped his hands, allowing her to step back.

"What is it, Cat?" he asked again.

She didn't know how to answer. The episode with Elena had hurt and angered her but, even so, his magnetism was strong and still pulled at her. Perhaps because she was tired, she found it very difficult to resist. "Let's say goodbye here. My house is only a few steps further."

Beck looked across a line of tall shrubbery to see the roof of a dwelling he hadn't noticed before. She started to pick up her case, but he forestalled her. "There aren't any lights on. I'd better walk with you." Even though she'd effectively turned him away, he was reluctant to leave her.

Catriona laughed. Her laughter came out sounding slightly hysterical, to him at least. "Have you forgotten where you are?" she asked. "This is Shared Ground. There's no danger here."

Not to you maybe, Beck thought. He was surprised at the feeling of protectiveness that rose in him. "There's the possibility of danger no matter where you are, Cat," he said aloud. "It's foolish to be careless about your own safety."

"But, Beck, this is Shared Ground." She repeated the name like a mantra, as though unable to believe he would be afraid for her in this place. "Maybe in other places, safety is an illusion, but here it's very real."

He pinned her with his eyes. "I know where I am."

She shrugged finally and led the way along the path to her house. "You'll learn to trust again, I suppose. If—" she shot him a quick glance and changed the emphasis "—*when* you return, if you stay for the full year, you will have a lot of things to learn."

"I'm sure I will," he responded noncommittally. She opened the front door.

Beck set her suitcase inside, said good-night and left. As he walked back through the garden, he felt as if he were already being torn in two directions.

Did he want to learn the lessons of Shared Ground?

He had one more stop to make. He veered off the main path, heading in the direction of the road. The sound of his footsteps preceded him, startling away the small night animals. There was no hesitation in his steps; he knew exactly where he was going.

The cemetery was in shadow but he found the graves of his parents easily, almost as though he had traveled this path dozens, hundreds, of times. In truth he had traveled it only twice since the tragedy seventeen years ago. Two days after the macabre double funeral he had come to say goodbye.

He took off his glasses and stood between the graves, head bowed, for a long, silent time. Gradually the night sounds resumed.

"Father, Mother, I miss you," he said softly.

He lifted his head, listening, blinking rapidly against the sting in his eyes. His voice dropped to a whisper. "I wish I knew what you would have wanted of me."

He heard the scurrying of a rabbit, the hooting call of a barn owl. And nothing else.

The serenity and peacefulness of this place invited him to linger, to relax as he retraced his steps along the neatly raked gravel pathways of the garden. All the worry and concern, all the exhaustion and frustration of the past weeks would have drained away—had he permitted it to do so.

But instead Beck concentrated on the arguments he was going to use, the explanations he would have to make, to the president. He amended that thought. He wouldn't be hard-pressed to explain; the man was desperate enough to try anything at this point.

Elena listened to her grandson's steps overhead as she prepared for bed. She moved slowly, cursing her old, tired bones.

When she had brushed her hair, cleaned her teeth and donned her nightgown, however, she sat down in a rocking chair beside a window that looked out over the garden. She knew that she should lie down, try to get some sleep. But she'd learned that the older she got the less sleep she required—or desired. The number of days and nights remaining to her was limited, and she did not enjoy wasting them in unconsciousness.

She probably didn't deserve it, but Beck had initially greeted her with all the love and affection of a beloved grandson. Then she'd dropped her bombshell.

After his antagonism had faded, he had again been gentle with her. But she knew that he was also adamant about his determination to return to Washington. If he stayed he would stay for the agreed time, but he would resent every minute.

What a fine man he had become. Her expression remained tranquil, even when her heart swelled with pride. Her son, John, would be proud, too. Her beautiful son, dead at so young an age.

She supposed that she had always focused too strongly on John. She knew that she was guilty of selfishness, and dismissive of Beck and his mother. And for seventeen years she had reaped her reward for her neglect.

She would never be able to recall the day of the accident without unbelievable pain. John and a group of men had been thinning trees on the north brow of the mountain. Lieda had taken lunch to the men. She'd been laughing at a welcoming remark, when she had stepped too close to the edge. The rock had been slick after a night of rain. She'd clutched at something—a tree, a shrub—and almost stopped her fall. John had made a grab for her. He missed and they both plunged to their deaths.

Tears welled in Elena's eyes, tears of sorrow for the loss of her son and his wife, for the mistakes she'd made with Beck, but also tears of gratitude that the last MacDomhall had finally returned home. Even though he'd had to be coerced, Beck was here.

Age was weakening her. The gifts that had been so strong in her youth were fading. She fingered her medallion. There was much he had to learn—much he had tried to reject and deny, much he continued denying. But she would have a year.

Elena smiled with genuine pleasure. She was looking forward to the confrontation between herself and Beck. She'd always relished a challenge and this one promised to be a dilly. Over the coming months, other factors would cloud the issue, but in the end the struggle would all boil down to them.

And Catriona, of course. She would not make the same mistake she had made with Lieda. Catriona was the necessity in the equation; Catriona was the catalyst.

Chapter 6

Darkness had not yet lifted from Shared Ground when Beck took his duffel bag out to the buggy...*car,* he corrected himself. He paused to sniff the clean morning air. No fumes, no toxins. Though his few hours' sleep had been restless, he felt surprisingly refreshed.

Despite his skepticism and doubts about a possible return to Shared Ground, he could not curb a sense of excitement as to the possibilities here. Clean air was a vital concern to the whole world; so the banishment of internal combustion engines by the community was only one of the progressive things to be studied—*if,* as Catriona had said, they had actually learned to store energy for long periods of time. He still had to be convinced of that.

Elena stood at the front door of the cottage, holding the picnic basket packed with the sandwiches he'd requested. Once he got on the road he didn't want to have to stop except for gasoline.

At breakfast Elena had introduced him to Janet, a quiet, youngish woman who lived nearby and came in daily to cook and clean for her. Janet was another adjustment in the life of the Gardener of Shared Ground. Seventeen years ago Elena wouldn't have tolerated anyone else doing her work. Janet's presence seemed to be the only concession she had made to her advancing years.

The basket also held the small but significant flagon that he was taking back to Washington. He didn't let himself reflect upon the contents, for now. There would be plenty of time for thinking when he was on the road.

He tossed the duffel into the back of the car and returned to Elena's side. He slid his hands into the pockets of his jeans and stood with his feet planted apart. His eyes met hers. The coach lights on each side of the door spilled across her upright figure.

"You are ready," she said.

The phrase was fraught with meaning that he chose to overlook. Though Elena stood two steps above him, he was still taller than she. But Shared Ground was her turf; she held the authority. The serenity of her features contrasted with his own sober expression. Now that the moment had arrived, he was imbued with disquiet.

Her features softened. She didn't go as far as a smile, but she came close. "Drive carefully," she cautioned. "I'll see you soon."

He took the basket from her hands and leaned down to kiss her. Once more he paused. "Elena—"

"I think Catriona has come to say goodbye." Without further comment she turned back into the house and closed the door.

He heard the click of the latch as he glanced at the road behind him. His heart gave a quick skip at the sight that greeted his eyes. Cat was striding self-confidently toward him out of the darkness. She wore white—slacks and a shirt in some soft easy fabric—giving her long-legged figure an ethereal quality.

To further complicate his inner turmoil, he'd spent a restless night on another, more lascivious, level dreaming of those long legs.

"Good morning," he said.

"Good morning," she replied.

A breeze pulled a strand of her hair free. She raised her arms to tuck it back into her barrette. The action lifted her breasts provocatively under the soft fabric. He frowned.

"All ready to go?" she asked, indicating the basket.

He forgot he'd been holding it.

"Ready as I'll ever be." He moved toward the car; she fell into step beside him. The scent of jasmine reached his nostrils; it would forever be her scent. He had a suspicion that for the rest of his life, whenever he smelled it he would think of her. He put the basket on the front seat. "When I get back, we have some things to discuss."

Catriona had told herself on the way here that she was a vacillating, weak-willed woman. She'd berated herself for the failing when she rose before dawn, scolded herself for impulsiveness while she dressed hurriedly, and lied to herself that she hoped he would already be gone.

But she'd found she couldn't let Beck leave without saying goodbye. She tried to explain the tingling in her belly by rationalizing that the entire community had a lot riding on this venture. The future of the garden, Beck's future, her own—all these were her justification for arriving unannounced in the wee hours of the morning to say goodbye. Again.

She did not know with absolute certainty that Elena's compound would work. If it did restore the president to good health, and Beck returned for his year in the mountains, then he'd be here under duress. She knew their goodbye would be uncomfortable for all those reasons and more, not the least of which was the most critical reason from her point of view—she mustn't let herself become emotionally vulnerable to this man.

She schooled her features into a semblance of detachment. "You'll have a busy year. I'm sure there will be plenty of discussions," she answered at last.

"Don't pretend to misunderstand me, Cat. You know what I'm talking about." Suddenly, as though against his will, he reached for her hand. Using a firm grip, he took her around to the driver's side of the car, which just happened to be in shadow.

Catriona was too surprised by the unexpected action to resist and then she didn't want to. His determination was clear—he was going to kiss her goodbye and she wasn't going to turn away this time. Little did he know that she had no intention of even trying. She felt her pulse accelerate in anticipation.

He came to a halt and brought her legs into full contact with his. He looked into her eyes for a long moment while their bodies shifted instinctively, her soft curves making subtle adjustments against his hard planes. He smiled his very masculine satisfaction and then lowered his mouth to hers.

The kiss on his patio during the storm had been an impulse; the kiss in the Washington park, an affectionate salute turned hungry. This kiss was long and deliberate, and very complete, everything a kiss should be, a comprehensive, unabridged kiss. His tongue swept through her mouth, demanding that she respond.

She wrapped her arms around his waist and let her head fall back when he moved from her lips to her throat. She clung; she couldn't have stood otherwise. His hand swept down her back to her hips, pressing her closer. The growing sign of his arousal crowded insistently against the juncture of her legs.

Suddenly he broke off the kiss and took hold of her shoulders to hold her away. His breathing was ragged and he bent slightly forward as he struggled for control. "Damn you, Cat. You make me want too much!"

And then he was gone.

Numb with longing, she stood very still and watched the object of her desire drive away. After a long time she finally turned away from the darkness into which he'd disappeared. Moving very slowly—she was sure that sudden action could cause her to shatter into tiny pieces—she turned toward another tunnel of darkness, toward her own house.

The numbness had barely worn off by the time she'd bathed and dressed and deliberately fixed a big breakfast—fresh blueberries, waffles with hand-churned butter and clover honey from Donovan Campbell's hives. And coffee, lots of coffee. She set her place at the table on the patio.

A family of robins had made a nest in the chestnut tree behind her house. The eggs had been laid in the spring, and two baby birds had hatched a few days before she left for Washington. She tried to use their antics to distract herself, but it didn't work.

Mentally she drove along with Beck. He'd have exchanged cars in the mountain cavern and made his way along the dirt track. Carefully. He might have even reached the paved secondary road.

The baby robins set up a racket. She smiled, listening. Their first-hatched cries of hunger had been tiny, weak things. During her absence, their voices had strengthened and the cries were more demanding. The poor beleaguered parents hustled, flying in and out of the branches of the old tree, nourishing the babies in preparation for their venture out into the big world. They only had a few weeks.

Surely Beck had arrived at the state highway by now.

Beck had arrived at the presidential retreat at Camp David the evening before. His first sight of the president after two days away had troubled him greatly.

Dark rings circled the man's fever-glittered eyes and his hands trembled. His skin had taken on a yellowish pallor, and his frame seemed more fragile.

Beck had tried to hide his reaction as they shook hands, but the president had known him for too long not to have read his shock and dismay.

"Sit down, Beck," the president said, his once-vibrant voice almost a whisper. "The doctors have already implied what your expression tells me clearly."

"Mr. President, I'm so sorry," Beck answered in a choked voice.

"I am sorry, as well. There are so many things left undone." The president moved his shoulders slightly in a weak parody of a shrug. "This job is demanding enough for a healthy person, for a sick one it is impossible. The sooner I step down the better it will be for the country. How was your trip?"

He settled into a chair beside the bed and leaned forward with his elbows on his knees, his hands, palms together, forming a tent under his chin. *This is it,* he thought. He steeled himself, anticipating the president's indignity. "Something of a surprise. The small town I left has become very... progressive. My grandmother is something of a visionary. She's sent..." He hesitated. Coward, he told himself. "She sends her best wishes for your recovery."

The man in the bed smiled with a show of some relief. "And what else did she send?" he asked.

Beck accepted the president's intuitive reaction. He was fast approaching the point where nothing about his grandmother really surprised him. "You knew she'd be communicating with you."

"In a way, I think I did." The president's eyes took on a faraway look. "They say that when you're near death, you see things ordinary healthy mortals can't see. I felt that something would come of your trip, Beck," he said. "A large measure of history is a consequence of luck or fate. Not a particularly reassuring thought, but true nevertheless. The right person with the right qualifications and preparedness is in place at the right time." He frowned and added, "Or the wrong one. But I sensed that there was a reason why you were called home this particular weekend."

"Sir, if you are strong enough to listen, I'd like to explain about the history of Shared Ground before I tell you the rest."

Beck knew he should keep the meeting as brief as possible, but he wanted to submit a full disclosure before offering the alkaloid compound. His boss—a dreamer, yes, but also a realist and a practical man—had to know some things about the background of the small Tennessee community.

"Go ahead," said the president.

Beck put aside his instincts, the tradition that had always dictated secrecy. For the first time in his life, he explained to an outsider about the history of the garden, about his grandmother and about Cat.

He tried to keep his explanation short; he could see that the man was exhausted. At last it all boiled down to one specific.

"If this works, I'll have many questions for you, Beck," the president said, "but I don't feel strong enough to ask all of them right now. Just tell me straight, if you think this—" he held up the vial Beck had given him "—compound will help me."

"Sir, I simply don't know."

"I've never known you to be less than honest, Beck. Will it do any harm?"

"No! My grandmother may be eccentric, but she would never harm anyone," he assured the man. "And—above all, sir, she *is* a trained scientist. The Gardener has always been qualified and experienced."

But then he hesitated. Elena was almost a hundred years old. What if her age had caused her to make a mistake?

No, she would never have given him the vial if she'd had the slightest doubt. Still, if the Secret Service ever got wind of this, he'd be dead meat. "I'd stake my life on her integrity, sir."

The president met his gaze. *That's exactly what you're doing.* They seemed to share the grim thought.

"Beck, if I had a choice, I might think twice. But I am growing weaker every minute." He made a fist in a demonstration of frustrated anger. Sick and weak as he was, the gesture was just that, a gesture.

But Beck was heartened by the attempt; the man was still a fighter.

"And, dammit, I have a lot to do." But then the man in the bed sighed; his fingers fluttered on the counterpane. "I'm going to take this compound. If it doesn't help me, I'll announce my resignation tomorrow. But I want to make it clear to you that taking the compound is my decision and mine alone. You are not, under any circumstances, to hold yourself accountable for my actions."

"Yes, sir," said Beck, but he knew that was a directive he wouldn't be able to carry out. He would be responsible, and he would live with that knowledge all his life.

And so that night, in the rustic cabin at the presidential retreat, Beck administered the compound to the president according to the directions Elena had provided. She'd warned that the patient would sleep for an extended period following the administering of the formula. Sure enough, the president had fallen into a deep sleep shortly after swallowing the contents of the vial.

Beck had left the cabin after telling the doctors that the president had fallen asleep during their conversation.

"He seemed strangely impatient for your return," said Hal, the doctor who was a close friend as well as physician. His look held a question.

But Beck didn't comment. He couldn't explain the president's premonition to himself; how could he explain to anyone else?

By nine o'clock the next morning, the presidential advisers had begun to grow antsy. When their boss hadn't awakened by lunchtime, they were almost in a panic.

The doctors continued to advise that rest was the best thing for him, but the cardiologist had begun to exchange worried glances with the endocrinologist. The urologist watched as the internist checked his pulse.

The president had not been able to sleep more than three or four hours a night for months. No one could explain this sudden change, but they continued to check his vital signs and agreed—all of them—that his slumber was the deep, healthy kind. They seemed cautiously optimistic.

Beck, on the other hand, sympathized with the other advisers. What in God's name had he done?

At last he left the dining hall where they'd all gathered to wait. He needed a walk to clear his head. He trudged the perimeter of the place, until, seconds later, he felt a sudden and inexplicable urge to return to his boss's side.

He took the steps in one leap, crossed the porch and paused to knock on the rustic wooden door. When there was no answer, he took a deep breath and reached for the latch.

The advisers were clustered at the door to the bedroom, and he could hear Hal talking excitedly. Then his ears picked up not the weak murmur of yesterday but the characteristically deep rumbling voice of the president. He hadn't realized how taut his body was until the tension snapped like a rubber band and he slumped against the wall in relief.

It had worked! Good God, it had worked! He didn't know what was in the compound; he didn't care. It had worked!

He straightened. Blindly he shouldered his way through the men until he reached the threshold of the bedroom and could see for himself.

The president looked up at his entrance. ''Beck, I'm glad you're here. Tell these fellows that we have to get back to Washington tonight.''

Beck stared at the scene before him; the president was sitting in bed, his back propped against the headboard. The return of his color alone was phenomenal. His complexion was pink, not a feverish pink, but the healthy color of good circulation, of wholesome blood running through his veins, nourishing his body. The lines that had scored his brow had smoothed somewhat, and the ones that bracketed his mouth had disappeared completely.

When Beck's eyes met the president's, an exuberant, if unspoken, message passed between them. The man looked ten years younger than he had when Beck left him last night.

One of the doctors was arguing, "Mr. President, we are all extremely grateful that you're feeling better, but you have been a very sick man. We all agree, strongly, that another few days of rest are essential for your continued improvement."

"I'm afraid I'd have to agree with the doctors, sir," Beck told him.

Elena had warned that the alkaloid compound would produce a sudden spurt of energy, but he should encourage the president to let his body have a few days to heal itself thoroughly before he plunged into the renewal of a full schedule.

"Very well," said the president. "I will remain here until Wednesday." He glanced again at Beck, his own expression enigmatic.

Beck gave him an imperceptible nod. Wednesday should be long enough.

"Beck, you'll stay, too."

"And me," said Hal firmly. But he was grinning. "You can't get rid of all of us that easily."

The man in the bed smiled at his friend's comment, then he turned back to the others and went on, "The press will be on us like ants at a picnic if we don't present the appearance of getting some work done. Arnold, you'd better get back to Washington," he ordered, speaking to his press secretary. "Tell them that Beck and I are working on a position paper." He grinned. "You, of course, are not permitted to reveal the nature of the paper. I will do that at a later date."

"Yes, sir," said the press secretary enthusiastically. "I'll leave right away."

Beck backed out of the room as the president continued to issue orders. There would be plenty of time later for a private talk. He went outside and sat heavily on the porch step.

God, he couldn't believe it! This compound from plants in a remote physic garden in Tennessee had changed the course of history. He took off his glasses and wiped his hand down over his face, exhaustion hitting him all at once. Drained of energy, he leaned his head against the railing and closed his eyes. The sunlight fell like a blessing upon him as he sat there, glasses dangling from his hand.

Slowly, one by one, the men left the cabin, stopping only to remark on the president's miraculous recovery. None of them, it appeared, questioned it. They were all much too grateful.

It was difficult to keep the crazy grin off his face when Roger Henderson joined him on the step. "Most amazing thing I've ever seen," said Roger. "I wouldn't have given him a month after he collapsed Friday." He shook his head in disbelief.

Beck realized suddenly that he had to diffuse the speculation. He shrugged in what he hoped was an off-hand manner. "The doctors were right all along, I guess. The president needed rest in the most desperate way and his body wasn't allowing him to get it. Maybe the collapse was what triggered his recovery."

Roger shook his head. "I don't know, Beck. I just don't know. After he regained consciousness, he was just as hyperactive as he'd been before. He couldn't sleep Saturday, either. According to Ken," he said, mentioning one of the Secret Service men who guarded the president, "his light was on all night."

"Well, 'ours not to reason why,'" Beck quoted lightly. "We can just be grateful for his recovery."

Roger rose. "Yeah," he said with a broad smile. "God, am I grateful!" As he ambled away, he added almost as though he were speaking to himself, "It sure is weird, though."

If you only knew, thought Beck.

That night Hal, Beck and the president had dinner on the redwood deck overlooking the pool. The president was dressed but his clothes hung loosely on him. The sight was a painful reminder to Beck of all they'd been through these past few weeks.

After they had finished, Hal gave the president a last blood-pressure check before leaving for his cabin. The president asked Beck to remain.

Beck looked at the doctor, who nodded. "Just don't stay up too late," the man cautioned.

When they were alone and Beck had settled into an easy chair, the president asked his first question.

"Now, Beck, tell me why you're wearing that dismal expression."

Beck chuckled. He hadn't had a minute alone with the president since he'd given him the compound last night, and there were many things to be discussed.

Besides, he hadn't mentioned his promise to his grandmother. Reluctant as he was to stir the waters right now, he knew this had to be said.

The president listened attentively as Beck talked more about the isolated community in the eastern Tennessee mountains. He asked dozens of questions, all of which Beck answered freely, and seemed fascinated by the ideas that had come well before their time—the power plant fueled by wind and water and sun, the simple shaving from the rare stone that activated it. The ability to store power for long periods particularly stirred his interest.

"Good Lord, the potential for that alone is incredible."

"My grandmother seems to have guided her community to a startling level of progress. Though we have never been close, I have to admit I admire her for her forethought. I didn't have time last weekend to delve into the innovations in the garden itself, but Cat tells me they're doing nutrient-enhancement studies, similar to the calcium-enriched orange juice and the vitamins in cereals that are on the market now. But they seem to have taken the concept a lot further. They can superfortify the growing vegetables and fruits, based on a blueprint for good health."

"This Cat that you speak of, she's important to you, isn't she?"

The question both startled Beck and prompted him to consider. How important was Cat to him? "I've known her since she was a child. I'm very fond of her," he evaded finally.

They talked for a few minutes longer. At last, Beck told the president that he was leaving Washington. "Elena insisted, and I gave my word," he finished. "A year in the mountains in exchange for the compound."

The president's eyes were clouded as he studied Beck over his tented fingers. "I can't say I'm pleased over this information, Beck."

"I'm not overjoyed myself, sir. I've no idea how I'll explain to the others." The president's staff had grown close over the years they'd been together. They were like a close-knit family. "My leaving at this time is going to be seen as desertion by some of them."

The president held up his hand. "Let me take care of that. I'll think of a plausible excuse for the others." He gave a sad smile. "As much as anyone, I have damned good reasons to appreciate the value of a MacDomhall promise. If you have to go, you have to go." He sighed. "Someday, I must meet this grandmother of yours."

"She has coercion down to a science," Beck said bitterly. He remembered teasing Elena about using blackmail to get her way, but there was nothing funny about it. Now that the time had come to fulfill his promise, he felt trapped again. "Dammit, we have too much to do for me to spend a year vegetating in the mountains."

The president studied him. "I will give you that she's robbing me of one of my valued natural resources. But if it hadn't been for her compound..." He let his voice trail off.

Beck felt the heat rise in his face. He straightened in his chair. "Sir, I didn't mean to suggest that it wasn't worth the price."

The president waved off his explanation. "I know you didn't, Beck. But I want a pledge from you as well. I presume she wants to make your stay a permanent one."

"She probably does," Beck admitted.

"Well, I want you to give me your word that you will return to your staff position after this year is ended."

Beck grinned, relieved. He wouldn't admit it to himself, but he'd been worried that someone else would fill his shoes so well that he'd be out of a job. "That's a promise I'll be happy to keep."

"How has your community been able to protect its privacy all these years?" he asked curiously.

"In my opinion, it's all been luck. John Mac-Domhall chose the site when he emigrated in the seventeen hundreds. The physical isolation of the community has helped, certainly, and the fact that we border the Great Smoky Mountain National Park. The boundary line between Tennessee and North Carolina is not far from the valley and sits exactly on top of the Smokies. The mountains there are older than the Alps, Himalayas or the Rockies and contain some of the last great hardwood forests.

"As for the community itself, I have to admit that to some it might be considered a small Eden. The Gardener is sort of a combination mayor and secretary of state," he added with a rueful grin. "There is an instinctive inclination on the part of the community to draw around that individual when the privacy of the community is threatened, to protect him or her."

The president was silent for a few minutes. "Beck, I think that the year you have committed yourself to spend in Tennessee might just be a blessing in disguise," he said thoughtfully.

"Sir?"

The older man considered. When he spoke again it was with determination in his tone. "Consider this year as a mission for the country, for me. I want you to bring back the scientific knowledge and technology the community has developed. We will be able to take the knowledge even further, as far as resources allow. This could be a blessing to the whole world, Beck.''

Beck agreed; however, he had some reservations that must have been reflected in his expression. He was relieved when the president added, ''You don't have to stress the importance of protecting the community, Beck, particularly the secret of the compound.''

''There are limitations to the process used to produce the compound. As my grandmother explained it to me, some of the alkaloids take years to process,'' he stated. ''I gather that it can only be produced about once every other generation. And only she has the formula. That fact alone makes secrecy imperative.''

The idea sobered the president. ''I shall have to be worthy of the distinction she has placed upon me,'' he said quietly. ''And you have my word that I will never reveal this secret to anyone.''

''I would never have thought to ask for your word, sir.''

''Can you imagine the public uproar that knowledge of such a formula would cause?'' mused the president, thoughtfully. ''In no time at all the place would be inundated with unscrupulous people. We will have to be very careful. Good God, Beck, we could end up going to war over this.''

Beck was relieved to see that the president's excitement had become severely tempered by reason. He'd not lied when he'd said that the man's word was unnecessary, but there were others, and even a hint—

''Now,'' the president said, rubbing his hands together. ''We'd better get to work to come up with a new

idea for a position paper. Something to satisfy the la-
dies and gentlemen of the press.''

"There is that compromise appropriation bill in
Congress . . .'' Their conversation moved on to practical
matters.

The man who had been listening outside the cabin
window faded into the shadows.

Chapter 7

T wo weeks later when Beck stopped the community car to stare out over the valley, it was late afternoon. The last time he and Cat had arrived it had been after dark— though there had been a moon—and he had left before sunrise the next morning. Seeing the town for the first time in daylight, the changes Cat had mentioned were more obvious.

He was surprised by the bustling atmosphere and the prosperity of the place. It was summertime and the children were out of school. He could see activity in the streets of the town, on the grassy softball field and at the lakefront beach. It looked as if they had extended the size of the beach and constructed a bandshell nearby.

He could also see that the boundaries of the garden had stretched beyond the original six acres. Two additional greenhouses had been built, and it looked as though work were about to begin on a third.

He caught sight of movement near what he remembered as the drying shed and shook his head, trying to quell the sudden lifting of his mood, to deny his pleasure at the prospect of seeing Cat again. Many times over the past two weeks—and against his will—his memory had called up vivid and elaborate images of her, of the graceful way she moved, her very individualistic scent, her smiles.

He'd had the devil of a time warding off those counterfeit images. She couldn't be as lovely, as appealing as he remembered.

Instead he concentrated on the depressing emotion that had traveled with him from Washington—a feeling that he was about to enter a cell. And the sentence was for a year, he thought pessimistically, a whole damned year in this isolated valley.

He sighed, took his foot off the brake and let the odd vehicle start down the mountain. But his interest was suddenly caught and he stopped again. His eyes scanned the road in front of him. The color was wrong, not the dull black of asphalt, not the dirty gray of concrete, it was instead a dark color, brownish, like devil's food cake. There was a sheen to the material.

He hauled at a lever, hoping it was the emergency brake, and got out. He knelt to lay his palm on the surface. It felt cool, not cold, just pleasantly cool to the touch, despite the heat of the day. The material was composed of millions of tiny beads not much larger than grains of sand. Interesting. He got back into the car and drove on.

A few people stopped to watch when the car, powered by its strange hum, passed through the village. Some were strangers to him, but he was surprised to realize that he recognized quite a few.

Nancy MacDougal, standing outside the schoolhouse with a paintbrush in her hand, cried out, "Welcome home, Beck." Nancy was a couple of years younger than he; she must be a teacher. He stopped and talked to her for a minute.

"Good to have you back," called Douglas Blaylock from his bench in front of the general store. Several of the men with him waved. Douglas must be almost as old as Elena, and he'd been holding court in that same spot for as long as Beck could remember. Some things never change.

Beck returned their greetings with a wave and a smile, but each salvo only fueled his irritation. Evidently his grandmother had announced his impending return to the community. But he didn't relish playing the prodigal. He steered the vehicle toward Elena's house.

Catriona and Elena were in the drying shed, sorting the plants Catriona had harvested earlier in the day. She'd been waiting expectantly, listening with her ears attuned for the hum of the car. A device in the cavern and another on the road announced visitors. She and Elena had heard the soft chime, like the sound of a clock signaling the hour, over fifteen minutes ago. Where was he? What if he couldn't get the car started?

Elena was talking, but suddenly Catriona no longer heard the words. Unconsciously she rose, clasping a nosegay of fragrant grasses to her chest. "He's here," she murmured. Her heart began to thrum in anticipation. She missed Elena's smile.

Quickly she recovered herself. Silly woman, she told herself. She scolded her pulse for its accelerated rhythm. She mustn't forget he was here under duress.

The two women met Beck at the door to the garden. His gaze flicked at once to Catriona but settled on his grandmother. "Hello, Cat. Elena."

Late at night on the day after he'd left, Cat had taken his telephone call, had passed the news of the president's recovery to Elena. She told the older woman that he needed two weeks to wind up his business. She didn't tell her of the resentment she could hear in Beck's voice.

Now Catriona noticed he didn't say "I'm home." She also noticed there was no affectionate hug, no smile for his grandmother. Or from her.

Though she was well aware that Elena was not an affectionate person, the total lack of warmth in the greeting annoyed Catriona for some reason. There were undercurrents going on here that she didn't understand.

He was poker-faced. His square jaw was thrust forward, his neck and shoulders were straight, as though he stood at attention. The expression in his eyes was impassive and chilling and . . . something else. As bleak as his expression had been when he thought his boss was going to die.

She felt a surge of compassion for him, followed by uneasiness. How could he accomplish what Elena expected of him when he was facing it like a punishment to be endured?

Mentally she shrugged and forced her gaze to the grasses she still held. Beck wasn't her problem; Elena would have to deal with him.

"Come inside," said Elena calmly. "You must be hungry. We'll have an early dinner."

Beck pulled off his glasses and rubbed his eyes. Elena looked at him sharply. "The first thing we have to do is get you started on treatment for your eyestrain . . . thyme and knotweed."

Beck replaced his glasses. "I beg your pardon," he said.

"Knotweed—*Polygonum aviculare*—strengthens and protects eyes. Thyme, is a good source of Vitamin A, which improves eyesight. Join us for dinner, Catriona."

Catriona had begun to enjoy Beck's confusion, but at the preemptory tone, her brows drew together. Then she shrugged, choosing to take the statement as an invitation rather than what it was—a command. "Thank you, I'd love to have dinner with you," she answered with a gracious smile.

Elena looked at her in surprise.

Beck's eyes glimmered with amusement.

"Let's go inside then," said Elena calmly.

They ate in the formal dining room.

Catriona wondered if that was Elena's notion of a welcome-home gesture.

To her dismay she found out that she'd been mistaken when she'd assumed Beck would be Elena's problem. After dinner, when the table had been cleared, the dishes rinsed and left in the sink for Janet to deal with in the morning, and she was about to take her leave, Elena opened the conversation that was to drastically alter her life.

"Now, let me tell you what I have planned," Elena said. She placed her hands on the table and looked from one of them to the other to make sure she had their undivided attention.

Though it was to Beck that Elena directed her words, Catriona felt absurdly like a schoolchild under the piercing gaze. "There is no time to be wasted. You have only a year. At your age that may seem like a long time, but at mine, I can assure you, it is not."

Catriona listened, growing more and more dumb-founded and dismayed, as Elena proceeded to map out the work she expected from them during the first two weeks. "Catriona will be teaching you the rudiments of specialized gardening. Then, depending upon the rate of your capacity, she can move on to—"

Catriona finally found her voice. "But—"

Elena's blue gaze swung to her, interrupting her objection. "Yes? Is something unclear?"

"I thought you . . ." She let the words trail off, which wasn't like her at all.

"You thought I would teach him as I taught you? There are other aspects of Shared Ground traditions that Beck will learn from me. But surely, you realize I'm much too old to traipse around in the garden all day, Catriona."

Catriona shook her head helplessly. "You expect me to teach him everything in one year that it has taken me many years to learn?" She was flabbergasted and she let it show. "That's impossible."

"Nonsense. You aren't dealing here with an ordinary student, Catriona," Elena reminded her pointedly. "For many years Beck has had to absorb and assimilate a tremendous amount of information in a limited period of time. I'm sure his ability is well developed by now. Besides, he doesn't have to know it all. You'll be here."

Catriona bit off another objection, but she was deeply wounded by the mandate. Obviously she was to train her own replacement. How easily Elena had dismissed her as having any claim to the job herself.

If she argued too heatedly with Elena's plans, she might reveal that she was faced with another, more instinctive problem. Being around Beck all day, every day, without betraying her own emotions was going to be very difficult.

At one time, in her early twenties, Catriona had longed for a permanent relationship, a husband or lover to share with, to love.

She had finally put those longings aside, sure that there was something lacking within herself. She had felt affection, fondness, even passion, but she had never felt love. In fact, she'd never quite reconciled the definition of the word. When she was very young, she'd assumed it was the giddy warmth described in novels. That had seemed like a very dangerous emotion to her.

As she'd gotten older, she'd begun to hope that love was an emotion that, like her plants, was enhanced in combination—a kind of superenriched strength, produced when two people together were more, somehow, than the sum of their individualism.

In Beck, she realized that here was a man who could provoke, if not the synergism, then giddiness.

She glanced at him. His pose was studiedly relaxed. His body was slouched, his broad shoulders resting against the chair back, his fingers laced casually across his hard, flat belly. He was watching his grandmother with an unreadable expression in his gray eyes. His power and masculinity were as much a part of him as his soul. She would have to be extremely wary and careful.

Beck's reaction to his grandmother's statement was a quick surge of suspicion. She was absolutely right. The president expected his assistants to present a clear, concise and correct evaluation on any given subject at any given time. The man chose his staff for the ability, and it was an invaluable talent, one Beck had carefully honed through the years.

He stood when Elena said good-night and left them alone together.

Catriona had risen, too. Now she walked slowly to the window. She crossed her arms at her waist and cupped her elbows in a self-protective gesture that he could easily understand. He drew a quick mental picture from the back of his mind—Cat, looking very professional, very capable, in the Washington park. She had been on a mission and was confident that she could achieve whatever she set out to do, even if it sounded bizarre to her own ears.

In sharp contrast to his memory, she stood looking out into the fading light. Her back, the straight spine, the squared shoulders, were the same but suddenly seemed very fragile and vulnerable to him. He had an urge to go to her, to wrap her in his arms, to reassure her that everything would be all right. At the end of the year he would return to Washington and she would go on here as before.

He knew how Cat felt about his return; she'd made her stand clear from the first. And now Elena had dumped more responsibility on her.

He'd done his best to assure her that his stay was temporary, but no matter how sincere his promise, he sensed that she still had reservations. Until the day he walked away from here, she would be unsure of her future as Gardener. It was a natural response; jealousy was a natural emotion.

Hell, he didn't know how to put it any more plainly. If she didn't believe him, she would just have to ride out the year. He opened his mouth, unsure of what he was going to say but knowing that he had to make some kind of protest on her behalf. Before he could form the words, however, Cat swung back to face him.

She dropped her arms and lifted her chin. "Very well," she said. "There is a lot to accomplish so we should get an early start. Can you be at my place at six?"

"Sure," he said.

"Okay." She hesitated, seeming to want to add something.

Beck met her clear green gaze, trying to convey his understanding.

He recognized his mistake immediately when she stiffened visibly in response. She'd misunderstood his expression as sympathetic. Cat was as strong as she was beautiful. She wouldn't want—hell, she wouldn't accept—sympathy. Such an emotion would offend her.

At last she broke off their eye contact, shrugged and went to the door. "I'll see you in the morning then. Good night."

"I'll walk over with you."

Catriona felt her blood heat, remembering the morning of his departure. The kiss they'd shared—she could still feel the pressure of his lips, the warm bond of his arms holding her, the hungry exploration of his tongue. She shuddered as that memory provoked instant arousal in her. She forced a lightness into her tone that she wasn't feeling. "It isn't necessary. As you can see, it isn't even quite dark outside."

But his eyes were. Suddenly, unexpectedly black dark, obsidian, telling her without words that he remembered, too. "I should get the books Elena wants me to read, shouldn't I?" he asked mildly.

Hot rose colored her cheeks. Beck thought her confusion was lovely.

"Oh, of course," she said. She opened the door, to be met with the pungent scent of a bayberry bush and the heady smell of ripening peaches on the small grove outside Elena's kitchen. He closed the door behind them and walked beside her in the rapidly deepening twilight. She inhaled deeply, but all the wonderful fragrances of the garden failed to soothe her as she'd hoped. She picked up her pace.

The last time they traveled the path, approached her house, she'd not invited him in. Tonight she had no choice. She entered her own cottage, motioning for him to follow.

Beck was surprised by her house. He wasn't sure what he'd expected, but it wasn't this hodgepodge of eclectic furniture that leaned heavily toward stark design. Not that the atmosphere was cold—indeed the pine forest seemed to have scented the whole place, and the colors she'd chosen to decorate with were warm—but the room was . . . unfinished somehow. That was the only way he could find to describe the place, untouched and unfinished. As though the room waited expectantly for someone to come in, toss aside a sweater, slip out of their shoes. The place looked as though she planned to be able to walk out at a moment's notice.

Was this a reflection of the sense of abandonment Cat was troubled by when she was a child? He would have thought she would have gotten beyond those feelings.

But maybe not. Maybe the sleek, sophisticated woman's image was only a veneer over the frightened insecure little girl.

He couldn't understand the discrepancy; her ambition, her determination to succeed Elena as Gardener didn't fit with all this. His eyes swept the room once more. It didn't add up.

Cat saw Beck's curious gaze touching her things. She shivered at the sensation that caused, as though he were touching her. "It isn't at all like your grandmother's cottage," she said unnecessarily.

A half smile tilted one corner of his mouth. "I have a feeling you're going to be a tough teacher."

The remark surprised her. She lifted a brow. "That's a broad evaluation to make from a quick look at my living room. Why do you think so?"

He had a feeling she wouldn't be flattered by his observation, and this wasn't the time to make her mad. "Every magazine, every paper, is exactly squared with the corners of the tables. Not a thing out of place, not a speck of dirt or dust to be seen. 'Perfection,' remember?"

She smiled in reluctant amusement, the first time she'd done so since Elena had shocked her with the news that she would be responsible for Beck's training.

The simple one-word motto had hung above the door of the principal's office in the elementary school—still hung there as far as she knew. Along with Mr. Mac-Donald's unsmiling, no-nonsense demeanor, that motto had terrorized the students into far better work than they had thought themselves capable of doing.

She looked around as though seeing her home for the first time. "I guess I am a bit of a clean freak. Like your housekeeper."

The sight of her soft smile stirred something in Beck. He shoved his hands into the pockets of his slacks to keep himself from reaching for her.

"You'd better learn to be one, too," she went on. "Elena won't accept less than pure sterility in the laboratory, perfection in the garden, and precision technology. I suppose the habits have spilled over into my home life. Come on, the books are in the study."

So, he thought, Elena had drilled this into her. Somehow though, he didn't quite accept that as the full explanation. He followed her through a door near the fireplace. Her study was a duplication of the living room. Except for the books. It was hard to remove the warmth from a room filled with books.

He wanted to see the rest of the place, wanted to know if her perfection extended to her very private, personal space, her bedroom, but he recognized that now would not be a good time to ask.

"Speaking of technology, tell me about the paving material."

Her beautiful eyes lit with emerald pleasure. "You noticed," she said as though pleased with a pupil.

Hell, he hadn't even started his studies yet, and he was distracted by her sparkle of enthusiasm. He wanted to put his hands on her. He sighed. It promised to be a long year. "Yeah."

"I believe I told you about our resolution to live on our resources?"

He nodded. "Yes, you did."

"Well, this is a new composite. Unlike all other paving materials the composition allows water to drain directly through so that it can return, as nature intended, to the underground aquifer instead of evaporating on the surface of concrete or asphalt. The stuff rolls up like carpet. It is pretty sturdy material, but repairs, if they are ever needed, can be carried out in about an hour. You simply cut the damaged area away and roll out a piece to replace it."

"Good God!" he said. "What's it made of?"

"That's the best part. Recycled plastic. Tiny spheres of silica and some other things. I'm a gardener, not a chemist or engineer. One of them could explain more fully tomorrow, if you like."

He looked thoughtful for a minute, stroking his chin absently. Finally he sighed. "I guess I'd better stick to Elena's schedule for now," he said finally.

Catriona was careful not to let her disappointment show. "Of course." She took a book from the shelf, added another and another, continuing until she had an armful of volumes. "This should get you started," she said.

He reached to take the books from her. The back of his hand made contact with the soft warmth of her breast.

Catriona froze. And so did he. They stood like that for an eternity, staring at each other. The blood coursing through her body set up an ear-pounding rhythm that drowned out all other sound in the room.

Suddenly she thrust the books into his arms and whirled away. "Don't touch me like that again," she said harshly, speaking over her shoulder.

"Cat, it was an accident," he said, laughing casually in an attempt to lighten the incident. He deposited the books on a chair and stood behind her, his hands settling on her shoulders. "Not to say I didn't enjoy it." He turned her to face him. "You're a beautiful woman and you already know I'm attracted to you."

She shrugged off his grasp and took a step, out of the reach of those warm hands, before facing him. "Beck, we both know you don't want to be here any more than I want you here. If you have some kind of crazy idea of making the best of a poor situation by having a sexual relationship to keep yourself from getting bored, forget it.''

Beck's expression closed to her like a shutter falling over a camera lens.

She knew an instant's regret for the unfounded accusation, but she paused only long enough to catch her breath.

But before she could continue, he spoke. ''You can try to believe what makes you feel safer, Cat, but you know as well as I do that chances are it's going to happen. We don't know when or where, but we have a year to spend together. You're only fooling yourself if you think we won't make love.''

Inside she was trembling, shaking like a leaf in the wind, and she was deathly afraid he would notice. She made fists of her shaking hands and planted them at her waist. ''It doesn't have to happen. I'm no longer a child and you're no longer my hero. We're adults. Adults can control themselves.''

''Sure,'' he agreed, with a cynical twist to his mouth. ''Like you just did when you blew up over an accidental touch.''

She couldn't argue with that. ''Then I'll have to work us both so hard we'll be too tired for games.''

''You'll do that anyway.'' The twist became an unpleasant smile that fueled her anger. ''You'll do your damnedest to wear me down.''

''You're absolutely right. I'm going to be a tough teacher. I'll make Mr. MacDonald look like the sugarplum fairy before I'm through. Can you handle it?''

He shrugged. ''We'll see, won't we?''

She indicated the pile of books on the table. "You'd better get started on your reading."

Beck picked up the books and followed her out of the study, through the living room and passed her at the front door without saying good-night. Cold and unfinished, that was her house. That was her.

What the hell did he care?

Chapter 8

Catriona tossed and turned until the sheets looked as though a large herd of buffalo had trampled across the bed. She wondered how she was going to survive the next three hundred and sixty-four days. She had overreacted—Lord, *had* she overreacted—to a simple accidental brush of his fingers against her breast. Even the memory of that fleeting sensation was enough to make her bones feel like warm gelatin as she lay staring at the ceiling.

Her only excuse for snapping at him was her fear that he would read her response to his touch and take advantage of it.

He was a sensual man; he must have had many lovers. Women would respond readily to his charm and masculinity, not to mention the ultimate aphrodisiac—power. And the women in Washington were beautiful, intelligent, more an appropriate fit for him than a mountain girl. She was surprised at how painful that idea was.

Finally she threw the covers aside. A slender, quarter moon painted a parallelogram of silver onto the bare oak floor. Drawn to the window, she propped one knee on the cushioned seat there and looked out across the garden. In the attic of Elena's cottage the light still burned.

Beck was reading. He'd had a long drive today, and she could guess how chaotic the past two weeks must have been for him. He had to be exhausted, and yet he was reading.

She sank onto the window seat and drew her legs up, wrapping her arms around them and laying her cheek across her knees. The light burned steadily and, as she watched his window, she felt her regret pile up until it took the form of one tear, one tiny bulb of moisture that overflowed her eye and trailed down her cheek and into her hair. She wiped at it.

She hadn't even asked him about the president's condition, she realized with a sharp pang of remorse—remorse not only for her behavior but also for Elena's. She thought again about the kind of homecoming they had given Beck.

There had been no open, welcoming arms to greet him after seventeen years. No fatted calf from the people who loved and valued him the most. Just an abrupt and heartless, "At last, you're here. Now it's time to get to work."

True, Beck had not tried to hide his bitterness and resentment about returning to Shared Ground. But she really didn't blame him for that. He had an exciting and consequential career; he was one of the important people in the world, one of the ones who could make a difference. The charm and splendor of community life, which she adored and could never think of abandoning, had been lost to him years ago through the hand of fate.

What could one day have mattered, one day to adjust to this drastic change in his life?

And yet he hadn't protested. He'd taken the books from her and gone back to his childhood dormer bedroom and settled down to read.

Catriona wished she could turn back the clock a few hours. It would ease her misery if she could welcome him again, genuinely, tell him how glad she was to have him home. She wouldn't overreact this time. She wouldn't look with horror at Elena when the older woman had said Catriona would have to teach Beck. She should have seen that coming, she added wryly to herself.

When he took the books out of her arms, she should have laughed lightly at the accidental, if electrically intimate, contact. Then she could have handled the coming weeks and months with aplomb. As it was, she would have to reestablish her own control. And that was going to be the difficult task.

Suddenly, her head came up, her eyes narrowed, focusing in on the house across the way. Another light had been switched on—the one downstairs in Elena's bedroom. She watched for a while, waiting for it to go off.

But it was the dormer light that was extinguished first. Then, after a brief few minutes, the downstairs light. The house on the other side of the garden was dark.

Catriona smiled to herself. Elena had had her own dose of remorse, it seemed.

Beck knocked on Cat's door at exactly 6:00 a.m. She opened the door, dressed in an oversized pink shirt knotted at her waist and denim shorts. He decided that the shorts had been designed specifically to distract him. Her long hair was caught up at the crown of her head with a rubber band, leaving the blond mass to swing enticingly across her shoulder. The sunlight was kind to the smooth skin of her brow and cheeks.

"Good morning," she said. She smiled, looking as if she were about sixteen.

He was surprised by the cheerful greeting and struck anew by the contrast between this woman and the woman in the Washington park.

"Good morning," he answered, sliding his hands into the back pockets of his jeans.

"Would you like some coffee?"

"Yes, if you have some."

"Come with me."

He nodded and followed her down the hall to the kitchen.

Catriona felt his gaze on her, but she was determined not to let his attention make her fidgety. She expected that the small social niceties could get her through these tough beginnings. Her response last night was history; she would not overreact again.

He wandered restlessly about while she got down mugs, then filled a cream pitcher.

"What's this?" he asked, running his palm along the smooth surface of the island counter in the middle of the room. "Elena has one in her kitchen."

She broke off what she was doing and came over to show him. The compartments rolled out from beneath the counter like huge drawers. There were five of them. "Everyone in Shared Ground has them. They're breakdown bins—glass, paper, aluminum, steel, plastic. The organic garbage goes into the community compost pile.

But the other things are broken down for recycling right in these bins. It's very efficient.''

He dipped his hand into the bin she'd opened, the one for plastic, and scooped up a handful of the same tiny beads that had been used to make the road. "What do you do with it then?"

"Some of the materials are used in the experimental work I told you about. We have a small facility that sterilizes the cans for reuse. Plastic never dies, so there are all sorts of things to do with it. We take the rest of it—the paper and the glass—to processing plants outside the valley, and bring it back to be used again. We don't have room here for all the facilities we need. But we're working on that."

During her explanation his expression remained noncommittal. She'd hoped at least for a word of praise for all they were doing here.

If she had another motive for her enthusiasm, she didn't let herself think about it.

She returned to her task, pouring coffee for them both. She sloshed some on the counter and wiped it up.

"Would you like—" She turned with the mugs in her hands to find him lounging in her kitchen chair, his jean-clad legs stretched out in front of him, crossed at the ankles. One arm was hooked carelessly over the back.

He looked ridiculously comfortable and she hadn't even heard him move.

Nervously she cleared her throat. So much for good intentions. She set one mug before him. Instead of joining him at the table, however, she leaned a hip against the counter. "Would you like something to eat?"

"No, thanks. Janet fixed breakfast." He took a swallow from the cup. "Good coffee. How long has she been helping Elena?"

Catriona thought for a minute. "About a year, I guess." She hesitated. "Beck?"

He looked up.

She made herself smile. "I'm sorry about last night. All of yesterday, really. We didn't give you a very warm welcome and—"

As he waved away her apology, a muscle clenched in his jaw. "I didn't expect one," he told her curtly.

Her smile faded; she was oddly thrown by the answer. "How is the president?"

She thought she saw a shadow of sorrow pass across his features, but when he spoke, his voice was even. "He's well."

"And the negotiations you were working on?"

He stared into the coffee mug. "That world will move along without me, Cat," he said heavily. He raised the mug to his lips, took two more swallows, then set it on the table with an emphatic thump. He stood abruptly. "Why don't we get started?"

She caught her breath. Suddenly he filled the room with his masculinity, too much masculinity.

He smiled then, reading her clearly, and not above enjoying her discomfort. "I'm ready when you are."

The garden was enclosed by a stone wall, designed more to define the shape and importance than to keep the people of Shared Ground out. Indeed, the main gates, of beautifully wrought iron, faced the street and were latched to restrict unaccompanied children, but they were never locked.

For the garden was a place for inspiration as well as cultivation.

Originally, six acres had been set aside, but now the size had doubled to accommodate the additional developmental cultivation.

Beck and Catriona entered through the gate near her house. He expected her to begin his instruction immediately. Instead she led him to the spot where a statue stood at the juncture of two wide raked paths and, without speaking, took a spot on one of the benches there. He smiled to let her know that he appreciated the detour and looked up at the statue.

The carved likeness of John MacDomhall, who had laid out the garden, gazed serenely over the colorful acres—rich and verdant greens, splashes of gold, lavender, saffron and gentian. A bronze tablet at the base of the statue named the man who had led the band of Scots Highlanders to the colonies. "Born, 1709—died, 1788."

Every child in Shared Ground knew the story by heart. Even before John's birth, his grandfather, a seventeenth century Beck, had helped design and build the University of Edinburgh's physic garden. John and Beck were links in the chain that stretched back further, back centuries, back to the Middle Ages.

Legend had it that somewhere in the dim mists of the highland mystery was a gypsy woman, who fell in love with a laird and gave him a child. He was married, so the child remained with his mother. But eventually the laird's wife died. He legitimized the child and gave him the name MacDomhall. The clan prospered and legend had it that it would do so as long as the name was retained. When the women in the family married, their husbands had to promise to take the MacDomhall name.

The twentieth-century Beck MacDomhall, sitting in the clear morning sunlight, reflected on his ancestors. In the peace of this place, he was finding it easy to give those ancients his attention. That was a strange development, he admitted to himself. In the past he'd never been particularly curious about them.

The MacDomhalls were a hearty lot, he'd give them that. And not afraid of work. As a child, one of his duties had been to gather mistletoe in November. He would shimmy up the trees, hickory, sycamore, mountain oak—wherever the largest bunches with the whitest, plumpest berries could be found. He then rode with his father across the mountain into the county seat and sold it to dealers at the railroad, who shipped it north for holiday decorations.

"I noticed when I came over the mountain that you've almost doubled the size of the garden," he said, suddenly breaking into the silence.

"We needed more space. Elena and I had added some plants that aren't of a physic nature. Some are rare and ornamental, nourishment and healing for the soul rather than the body." She gave an abashed smile. "Her words."

Rare and ornamental, thought Beck, an apt description of Cat. "Did you know there's a physic garden in Chelsea?" he asked.

She turned to him. "Yes, I've been there. When I was in college one of my professors took a group over. Have you seen it?"

He nodded. "Last summer when the president went to Britain to meet with the prime minister," he answered.

Catriona was bewildered by his admission. The general public wasn't too interested in physic gardens. The one in the middle of London was there because a lease had been granted in 1722 by the owner of the manor on condition that the area remain a physic garden. The city had grown dense around the plot.

She wanted to ask Beck why, when for years he'd disavowed any contact with his background, he'd bothered to visit the garden in Chelsea. She held her tongue, however, and was rewarded with the information without having to ask for it.

"I don't know what drew me to the place. I don't even think I knew it existed. But I overheard someone mention the physic garden along the Chelsea Embankment so I thought I'd go have a look. You know, Cat," he continued thoughtfully as his gaze traveled the path in front of the statue, "it can't hold a candle to this place."

"Because of the city's pollution," she explained sadly. "In fact they're doing some important studies there on the effect of pollution on plants. That's why our professor took us there." She sighed and looked around. "Though our winters are severe, we're very fortunate here. The valley is somewhat protected from really harsh weather by the mountains. And our air and water are clean."

Spontaneously she rose and began to pace. He hid a smile, her pacing was a habit he enjoyed. She moved so fluidly, so gracefully. Finally she came to a stop in front of him. "We're getting about more. More people travel, I mean. I myself traveled to South America with a group of botanists and horticulturalists two years ago. We rescued plants from the Amazon Delta in hopes of finding future uses for some that were in danger of extinction. It saddens me to think that possibly some of the plants that grow along the shores of the river could hold cures for devastating diseases, but they may be lost to us forever."

She seemed nervous when she talked about travel, and he wondered why. "I'm familiar with the expedition, but I didn't know you had gone with them." He laid his arms along the back of the bench, hooked his ankle over the opposite knee and looked up to study her for a minute. "I'm curious, Cat. Shared Ground used to be almost totally isolationist. The people left to go to college and came back, occasionally bringing a new spouse, even rarely deciding not to return. But people didn't do much traveling once they were full-fledged adults. It seems to me now that you get around a lot more. Tell me, what's brought on this trend?"

Catriona tried to shrug off his observations, but he persisted and finally she answered. "It isn't really a trend, thank God. I hate it. Most of the others prefer to stay here, too, as we always have."

"Then why travel?"

"I can't pretend to second-guess Elena, but I think she simply decided it was time that we helped out where we could. The world is shrinking, and it faces a lot of problems. We may have the answers to some of them," she answered. Then she dropped her eyes under the force of his gaze. "Or maybe it was your leaving that prompted the turnabout. She knows that we have to move with the times. The technological advances—"

He interrupted. "It won't work, Cat," he said harshly.

She stared at him. "I don't know what you're talking about."

"Don't you? I told you last night that we would stick to Elena's plan for now. You keep pushing all these enthusiastic explanations about the developing technology. It is as interesting to me as you knew it would be. More so than the garden.

"But don't try to divert my attention to the technological advances. Don't barricade yourself against me. Elena wouldn't stand for it, you know."

Catriona never lied to herself; she considered that the worst dishonesty of all. Jaw agape, still staring, she sank onto the bench beside him. "Is that what I'm doing?" she asked weakly.

"Looks like it to me."

Dear God, she hadn't even known that her subconscious could be so devious. "I didn't mean..." She swung away. "Maybe I did, but not consciously." She was deeply embarrassed, but thoughtful.

He remained silent, but, when she rose and started down one of the paths, he followed. She would have preferred being alone. The next best thing would be to get to the greenhouse where her work waited.

Unexpectedly he took her hand and brought her to a halt. "There are a lot of complications in this situation, Cat. I think we'd better talk. Is the belvedere still there?" he asked, mentioning the lookout that sat on a grassy plateau about halfway up the side of the mountain.

"Yes," she answered quietly. But she sought an excuse. "Elena—"

"Won't care if we take some time off," he finished for her, smiling a little. "Let's go up there for an hour or so." When she still hesitated, he tilted her chin with his hand, looking into her eyes. "Trust me on this, Cat. The lessons will go more smoothly if we try to find a route around some of these problems."

"All right."

They walked side by side in the warm morning sunlight, their sneakers making soft scraping sounds on the pebbles. Soon they left the garden, moved into the shadowed coolness of the forest and began the gentle climb.

After ten or fifteen minutes' walk, they finally emerged into the sunlight. At this height a stiff breeze was blowing.

The old belvedere, with its waist-high walls and rounded pillars, had been built of stone. The structure perched on the brow of the ancient mountain like an eagle about to take flight. The original thatched roof had long ago been replaced by a tin one.

Catriona waited for Beck to speak, her hand still sheltered in his. She knew, from years ago, that he considered the belvedere his sanctuary.

Many times, as a child, her shorter legs had taken her scrambling up the slope after him. If he said it was okay, of course. Never would she have intruded on his solitude without permission, and never would she have asked him to slow down.

They stepped into the shelter. On the hard-packed dirt that was the floor their shoes made no sound.

Beck gave her fingers a squeeze and released her hand. He walked to the low wall and, straightening his arms, leaning forward, he placed both hands on it, about three feet apart. He moved his head in a slow 180-degree turn, his gaze sweeping across the mysterious beckoning land, with its undulating mountains, dense forests, thick undergrowth, jutting crags and the dreamy blue haze, the veiled mist that gave the great mountains their name.

A distant waterfall shimmered silver in the sunlight. "The view never changes," he said.

Catriona watched the effects of the refuge upon Beck's features with fascination. Slowly calm seemed to settle on his brow, his cheeks, his strong jaw, smoothing lines, easing worry. Curiously she felt a matching contentment descend upon her.

"You were right to insist that we come here," she said softly, earning herself a brief, over-the-shoulder smile, before he turned back to the view.

"It's a good place to think, to get a clearer perspective on things," Beck agreed. All his senses were engaged. The view was spectacular. The scent of pine was strong on the air and, warmed by the sunlight, the ancient stone was rough under his palms. He felt his spirits being lifted in harmony with the bird songs and the humming of insects.

Catriona sat on one of the old stone benches. She hooked the ends of her sneakers on the edge and wrapped her arms around her knees. She tilted her head against the edge of the wall behind her and waited patiently while he absorbed what he seemed to need from the belvedere.

It was an unexpected pleasure for her to be able to watch him without being observed herself. The contrast to the man in Washington was amazing. His hair was a bit overlong now. His jeans were well-worn and faded in the interesting places where jeans always seemed to fade. They fit him closely, like a comfortable old ally. The cotton shirt, a dress shirt with the sleeves folded back to the elbow, looked worn and soft, too.

She let her eyes roam freely across his broad shoulders, the prominent muscles in his arms, his lean hips and waist, his strong thighs.

At last he turned. He rested a hip on the wall and crossed his arms. "Now, Cat. About us," he said.

Her misgivings returned, but this time Beck was all business.

As she listened she felt a certain diversion. He laid it out for her in a soliloquy that would have been a credit to a fine Shakespearean actor at his most eloquent.

He began by telling her that he would like to spend today wandering around the town, maybe go out to the countryside. He wanted her to go with him. He'd been away for so long, he explained, he was going to have trouble with names, and of course, there were a lot of new people to meet.

She agreed. And after last night, as he had realized, Elena would, too.

After today, he had a lot to accomplish in a limited amount of time, he said. The belvedere would be neutral ground. If they ran into snags in their relationship—arguments, problems—they would come back up here and talk it out. She nodded.

He went on. They couldn't let his resentment at having to leave Washington or her jealousy of his position in Shared Ground stand in their way.

This time Catriona's nod was slower in coming.

"I don't know how we will handle the physical attraction," he told her almost casually. Then he looked at her through lowered eyelids and his voice dropped an octave. "You're one hell of a sexy woman."

Suddenly her mouth was dry. If she were to teach him, she told herself, she would have to maintain some distance. But how could she, if he made remarks like that?

Before she could speak, he continued, "However, if you won't make it a habit to wear shorts like the ones you're wearing this morning, I'll try to keep my mind on the job and off your... off you." He cleared his throat. "I'm not promising anything," he went on, "but I will try."

He had caught her unaware. She stared at him as though he'd grown another head while she tried to think of something to say.

Then he began to chuckle, the unfamiliar sound percolating from deep within his chest.

"You're teasing, I hope." She narrowed her eyes to demonstrate disapproval but, despite her resolve, her lips twitched in response.

Fascinated, she watched a masculine slash appear in his cheek. The expression changed his whole face, his entire demeanor. He looked younger, reconciled to his fate, in fact, happier about the whole thing.

She had an idea that a resentful Beck would have been much more easily dealt with.

"You always were easy to get the drop on," he reminded. "But I believe in being honest. I'm only half teasing."

"Okay. I can live with your suggestions," she said mildly, refusing to furnish him with any further reaction. "All of them."

They didn't shake hands on the arrangement. An arm's length separated them as they walked back down the mountain.

When they reached the bottom, Beck sighed. It was going to be a very long year.

All day the wind had pulled at Catriona's hair and the sun had sought out the tender spot across her nose that burned so easily. She, who always kept herself neat and presentable even in her gardening clothes, was hot and sweaty. Her white sneakers were a dingy gray from tromping through the fields in Beck's wake and her clothes were a wrinkled mess.

The first thing he'd wanted to see was the boulder, the mysterious piece of stone that served as an ignition key for their vehicles. "Where have you put it?" he asked.

"It's right where it has always been."

He was visibly stunned by that. "What? You mean Elena hasn't taken steps to protect it?" he demanded angrily.

"I can see that we should have stayed in the belvedere," she said ironically. "Protect it from what? The people who use a bit of it almost every day? A little rain? The sun? We don't know that it isn't the elements that give it power."

He stalked off toward the corner of the garden where the stone had sat for almost three hundred years. She had to hurry to catch up with him. When he reached the spot, he stood looking down at the stone, nestled comfortably amid the white and pink rhododendron. At last he turned away with a sigh. The stone wasn't mentioned again.

They'd spent the rest of the morning driving around the valley. She'd let him drive. Then they'd had an impromptu picnic lunch on the small island in the center of the lake. He'd let her paddle the canoe.

But, as she looked on while Beck charmed yet another of their neighbors, she realized that she didn't mind the sunburned nose, or any of the rest of it for that matter. Today had been fun, and watching him in action was an education.

The people who remembered him didn't need charming. He was the MacDomhall.

The people who had joined them since he'd left were slightly wary at first. But he soon disarmed them with his easy smile, his quick wit, his genuine interest.

Suddenly she realized that he had spoken to her. "What?"

He grinned. "Pay attention here, Teach," he teased amiably. "I was telling Virginia that you used to like to throw a pot or two."

She looked blank for a minute. Then she smiled politely, looking up from the lovely cachepot she held in her hands. The pottery shop was filled with beautiful things—trays and plates, bowls and mugs, vases and unique figures.

Virginia West had only been in Shared Ground for a year or so but, as an apprentice potter, she showed an impressive talent for the craft. Her expression registered surprise. "Really?"

Catriona replaced the bowl carefully on the shelf next to an entire matching dinner set. She wondered how Virginia had managed the magnificent sky-blue glaze. She recalled that the blues were among the most difficult colors to produce with consistent shading. "Yes. I really enjoyed working with the clay," she said wistfully. "I wish I still had time."

A shadow crossed Beck's eyes. "Thanks for showing us around, Virginia," he said, some of the pleasure now missing from his tone.

"Anytime, Beck," Virginia answered. "Catriona, if you decide you'd like a turn at the wheel, you're always welcome."

"Thank you, Virginia," she answered absently.

The sun had disappeared when they left the shop. It was dinnertime and the streets were almost deserted. Beck took only a few steps before turning to face her. He was clearly irritated, and Catriona was at a loss as to any reason why he should be.

"Let me ask you something, Cat. How long has it been since you took a day off?"

"What?"

"Why *don't* you have time for throwing pots?"

"Beck, this is ridiculous. You don't—"

"Understand? Right you are." He frowned and whipped his glasses off. Without them, his eyes glittered. "You're supposed to be living in utopia. Why don't you have time to do the things you love to do?"

Her irritation rose to meet his. She took a step that brought her almost toe-to-toe with him. She put her hands on her hips. "I love the garden," she told him.

"The responsibility consumes your life," he accused. "The garden, Elena." His gesture encompassed the entire valley. "And now, me."

"I don't care. It's my life." She realized how childish her answer sounded. "I like it like this," she added.

The tinkle of a bell interrupted. Catriona swiveled her head to see Virginia eyeing them with interest as she left the pottery shop.

She realized then how foolish they must look, standing in the middle of the sidewalk, arguing like immature adolescents. And after spending such a nice day together. "Look what you've done," she snapped.

Suddenly he became very still, his eyes fixed on her face but focused somewhere else. At last he gave a ragged sigh and hooked an arm around her neck. "Ah, hell.'' Gently he pulled her forward, and she felt the touch of his lips on her brow.

The kiss was insignificant, a brotherly kiss, but his lips were warm.

"Let's get out of here before we have to make two trips to the belvedere in one day," he said solemnly. Then he turned with her still under his arm and walked slowly down the street toward her house.

Chapter 9

During the next few weeks, as they worked side by side, Catriona became so aware of Beck on a personal level that her perception seemed to pick up on every nuance of his progress. This had never happened to her before, this awareness of another person, almost as though she were inside his head.

She knew, for instance, without looking, when his expression evolved from interest to curiosity, and finally to amazement as she passed on bits and pieces of her knowledge of growing things. It was a transition she noticed often during his rapid development from novice to apprentice.

Beck's mind was keen. From the first day, she realized that he wouldn't waste a lot of time resenting what he couldn't help. Instead he used his energy and power to learn.

His intellect astounded her. He absorbed and formulated information like a sponge. The more mundane chores like weeding, potting and transplanting took up a lot of time. Once he mastered them—and he did so almost immediately—the time spent on the mindless physical tasks became the opportunity to hit her with a barrage of questions. It wasn't long before she found herself having to push to keep up with his unbounded curiosity.

She noticed other things, as well. One morning they were working in the shade of a lovely Chinese willow near the back of the garden, when Beck's head jerked around toward the direction of the road, not visible from where they were. Instantly he rose. "Back in a minute," he murmured and strode off along the path.

Curious, Catriona followed. She found him on one of the intersecting paths, hunkered down to put himself on an eye level with a little girl. Catriona looked around for an adult. Then she realized what had happened.

The child had gained access to the garden somehow. The garden contained many sophisticated plants. Drugs were produced from some of them. A few were poisonous if consumed; that's why the prohibition of unaccompanied children in the garden. Her heart skipped a beat.

Beck was talking quietly to the child and in answer to his question, she took one of his fingers in her small hand and led him in the direction of the front gate. A dogwood tree, planted outside the wall, had grown tall and strong enough for a child to climb.

"I'll take care of this right now," said Beck grimly, when the child had been carefully warned and had scampered off down the street. He headed for the tool shed.

Catriona was seized with a thought. "How did you know she was there?" she called to his retreating back.

Beck stopped in his tracks, but he didn't turn to face her. The broad shoulders moved carelessly. "I don't know. I must have heard something."

But Catriona hadn't heard anything and her hearing was very acute.

Another time, she had read into the night in preparation for the next day's lesson and awoke with a splitting headache. With her breakfast she took a mild prostaglandin-blocker made from vervain, a spiky plant with lovely lavender blossoms.

By the time she met Beck at the greenhouse, she had forgotten her pain.

He had been here for a while, it seemed. He'd loaded the wheelbarrow with established pine seedlings and the tools to plant them. He wore khaki pants, old ones that had been washed so many times they were almost white. His lightweight T-shirt was already wet from perspiration and defined the muscles in his arms. His dark hair hung over his forehead in damp strands.

After they'd said good morning she added, "You look like you could use a cold drink." Without waiting for him to respond, she went into the greenhouse and brought out two cans of a fruity soft drink that she loved.

He eyed the can—she knew it looked strange to him. It was painted an unadorned white, had no brand name, no logo, and was warm in his hand.

She smiled. "I keep a supply in the greenhouse."

"I thought you said cold."

"Pop the top," she instructed.

She tore the tab off her own can and smiled. "Now count to thirty."

"One, two, three—"

She laughed. "You don't have to count out loud."

Seconds later, she took a swallow. He watched her, then he raised his can to his lips.

An almost comical surprise registered on his face. "It's cold. And good. Tell me about it."

"The can is really two cans, one inside the other, with carbon dioxide gas in the space between them. Like dry ice," she explained between swallows. "When you pull the tab it activates the cooling process. Great for picnics and for saving energy. You don't have to refrigerate them." She set the empty can aside to take to her house later. "The formula for the drink is mine. I'm glad you like it."

"I can understand the principle, but who came up with the idea for the can?" he asked, turning it in his hand.

"One of the fourth-grade teachers has a small metal-working shop. It's a hobby with him." She laughed again and eyed him over her shoulder. "I wish you could have seen your face. We *do* have fun here, you know, Beck."

He drained his drink and placed the can beside hers. "I love to hear you laugh," he said easily. Then he added, "Your headache must be better."

Taken unawares, she dropped the burlap wrapping she'd picked up and whirled to stare at him. "You're doing it, too," she said faintly.

He had grasped the handles of the wheelbarrow and was on his way out the door. "Doing what?"

"My headache was gone before I finished breakfast. How did you know I had one? You see things—just like Elena does."

He froze for a moment, so brief she might have imagined it. Then he glanced back over his shoulder impatiently. "Don't be ridiculous, Cat. I just used my powers of observation. You were pale when you came in, and you still have a pinched look around your eyes. Forget it." He left the wheelbarrow outside and came back to heft a bag of organic fertilizer on his broad shoulder, as effortlessly as she would have lifted a pot of violets.

She tried to forget what she'd learned about Beck; she really did try to put it out of her mind. Because the idea of working around someone—a male someone—who might be able to read her thoughts was disconcerting. He might try to deny his power, but the signs were unmistakable to Catriona because she was accustomed to them, having worked with Elena for so many years.

The teaching experience was stretching her own capacities, as well. She'd not realized how specific her interests had become and how she'd neglected anything outside her particular field. She'd grown limited in her vision.

Beck still grumbled about her being a slave driver, but the grumbling had become more good-natured than hostile as they shared the excitement of learning and enrichment. As the camaraderie grew between them, she admitted to him one day that he was opening up new vistas to her.

He grinned. "Just wait." And there it was again—the sexuality that so strained her composure. The damnable thing was that she wasn't sure he meant the comment to be suggestive.

After five weeks had passed, Catriona discovered she no longer worried about his being able to digest everything in one year; now she worried that there wouldn't be enough to keep him busy. He was demanding in his pursuit of knowledge.

Of course, there was always the technological side of the community for him to explore. But she wouldn't be the one to suggest that. He'd accused her once of trying to steer him away from the garden; she wouldn't give him the chance again.

Though several times she had turned to find his eyes on her, fixed in an odd expression, there had been no moments of intimacy. Not on his part, at least. He was too busy.

Catriona's own feelings were another matter. She became more aware of him than ever, more sensually aware—observant of his physique, his gestures. Once or twice, when he stripped off his shirt to give himself freedom of movement for a task that required it, or if they took a cooling-off swim in the lake after work, she caught herself mooning over him like a silly adolescent.

And she wasn't the only one. The lake was a favorite gathering place on hot summer nights. Shared Ground had its quota of lovely, unattached young women who were clearly attracted to him.

He surprised her. His affability couldn't be faulted, but he kept a certain distance. Just as he did with her.

The tension grew within Catriona. She recognized it for what it was, but she was powerless to fight it. They hadn't had occasion to return to the belvedere. Perversely she found she missed the electric current that had linked them by invisible strings and produced the slight but interesting friction.

She could barely fault his concentration when that was his purpose for being here. He worked hard, his attention focused on the things he had to learn; indeed, he barely seemed to stop for breath. She told herself she was reconciled to the situation. And she avoided Elena like the plague. The older woman would know immediately that she was attracted to Beck.

Finally, one evening in mid-August, after the sun had disappeared over the horizon and when she least expected it, Beck stopped acting like her pupil.

They hadn't seen rain for ten days, an odd occurrence for the Smokies, where morning mist and evening showers were common all through the summer. Old-timers swore that each August day that began with early-morning fog was a harbinger of a winter snowstorm. If that was true, they were in for a decidedly mild winter.

Beck and Catriona worked side by side in the herb garden that evening, soaking a few fragile plant roots that needed additional water to restore the moisture baked out by the sun's scorching rays.

There was an outdoor concert tonight. From the band shell near the lake, the music floated easily over the garden. Later there would be the traditional bagpipes, but right now it was Mozart. Something happy, with the horns.

Mingled with the distinctive scents of the herbs was the clean smell of soil. A clear, sharp quarter moon had risen, giving out just enough light for them to see their way. With the onset of darkness, however, the definition of leaves and stems was becoming blurred.

Beck had been acting peculiar all day, his mood more casual than she'd seen it since his return. He'd laughed this morning—a big, hearty, I-really-enjoyed-that sort of laugh. Usually they worked comfortably together, and by the end of the day they were pleasantly tired. Tonight, though, there seemed to be an undefined restlessness in him.

Shared Ground performed a certain subtle magic on people, and she'd been pleased to note the changes over the past weeks. He had slowly adjusted his rhythm to the rhythm of the community. The serious, sober-minded man in his button-down shirts and hand-tailored suits had become encouragingly sloppy. The uptight, dynamic man was, occasionally, relaxed and philosophical.

But this restlessness was something else.

She rocked back on her heels and looked at him. He knelt on one knee, and one forearm lay across the other, his hand dangling, except when he had to push aside the leaves of a tiny, fragile plant to get to the roots with the hose. Then his hand touched the foliage as gently as a cat's whiskers.

"When I saw you in Washington, do you know what I thought?" she asked suddenly.

He glanced up, his white teeth flashing at her through the darkness. "No. But I have a feeling you're going to tell me."

She took her time. She stood up and dusted her hands off, then she wiped them on the legs of her pants. When she looked down at him, her expression was very serious. "I thought that you were a man who seldom smiled and never laughed."

He was quiet for a minute, his smile slowly waning. "I may have been that kind of man," he admitted thoughtfully. "It's a busy life, not a lot of time for laughing."

"You've laughed a lot lately."

"Maybe I'm becoming reconciled to my fate," he answered, teasing again.

"Perhaps. But if you went back to Washington tomorrow, Beck, you would be better for this experience."

"We'll never know, will we, since I'm not going back tomorrow."

She was surprised because there was no bitterness in his tone, none at all. "That's enough for tonight," she told him, stepping from between the rows onto a side path. "You could probably catch the end of the concert, if you like."

"What about you?"

"I'm grubby and tired and longing for a cool shower and my bed." She brushed her damp hair off her forehead with the back of her hand, leaving a streak of dirt. She sighed. "It's so darn hot. I'll be glad when this weather breaks."

Still hunkered down, with the hose in his hand, he looked up at her. A gleam of devilment appeared in his eye. "I can cool you off, Teach." He grinned and turned the hose on her, covering one segment of the nozzle with his thumb so the stream of water gained additional force.

"Beck!" she squealed, and jumped back. But she had never been one to run from a challenge. She suddenly grabbed the hose about four feet from where he was holding it and yanked it from his unsuspecting grasp.

"Hey, you rascal!" He came up to his full six-foot plus and headed toward her.

Laughing, backing away, she turned the nozzle on him. She began with his face, but he just wiped the water away and kept coming. She worked her way down his body until he was as wet as she was.

Of course, even the bravest challenge-facer knows when it's prudent to run. She dropped the writhing hose and whirled. She'd gained only a few yards when she was lifted off her feet by a muscular arm around her waist.

"The dream of every student—to finally have his teacher in his power. But now that I have her, what do I do with her?" Beck growled as he strode down the path.

Catriona tried to squirm free, but her laughter hindered the force of her attempts. "You put her down?" she suggested, still laughing.

"Yeah," he said softly. There was something odd in his voice.

He had reached a grassy berm near the greenhouses. Fireflies scattered as he stood her on her feet and stepped away, holding her gaze steady with his own.

They stood a foot apart, no longer touching. "Beck?" she whispered.

His eyes spoke for him, but he uttered the words anyway. "I want you quite desperately, Cat."

Her wet body reacted fiercely, as though she were joined to him by an electric arc through the air.

The French horns from Mozart's concerto approached crescendo.

The night seemed to hold its breath, waiting.

He stood with his feet apart. She saw his chest expand. Moving like a man in a dream, he slowly raised his hands and held them up, palms extended toward her.

His posture demanded a response. And the response was dictated by his stance.

She hesitated, sparing a thought for the setting—the world still intruded. But her hesitation lasted only for a heartbeat. She raised her own hands and put them flat against his.

He smiled his satisfaction, as though he had suddenly become the teacher and she was now his very superior pupil. His fingers slid into the spaces between hers. They stood that way, hand to hand, for long moments.

As a means of silent communication, thought Catriona breathlessly, it was very compelling. She felt as though he were speaking to her through her hands, as though his thoughts and emotions were being conveyed through the unique palm lines of life and health and love.

And then she was in his arms, crushed to his broad, hard chest. Suddenly—at last—his mouth was on hers. She parted her lips to take his thrusting tongue and worked her arms free to wrap them around his neck. A soft, keening sound escaped from her throat, and it seemed to ignite him further.

He cupped her bottom, lifting her, moving her hips against his hard arousal. A soft sound that might have been a bobcat's growl escaped from deep in his throat.

The light cotton shirts they wore, wet as they were, and the wispy lace of her bra were no barrier to the wild heat. But she didn't want even the skimpiest buffer between them.

As though she had spoken her frustration aloud, he broke off the kiss, stripped his shirt over his head, then disposed of hers. And then he stood looking down at her in the moonlight.

The illusive fireflies had returned. She could see them beyond his shoulder. But, she thought fancifully, they were no longer fireflies, the tiny luminaries became a frame for the setting, like moving starlight.

He closed his eyes for a brief second, visibly striving for control. Then he opened them again and, moving slowly, raised one hand to cup the side of her face.

"You are so beautiful," he murmured as he traced one satin strap with the fingers of the other hand.

Suddenly the intensity of her feelings frightened her, made her sway on her feet. The hungry desire that surged through her body was too mercuric, too unstable, almost savage in its intensity. She squeezed her eyes shut, instinctively turned her face into his palm, seeking not passion but reassurance.

Beck immediately sensed her anxiety. "Don't be afraid, sweetheart," he said soothingly. "I would never hurt you."

"I know you wouldn't," she said, her voice sounding more steady than she felt.

"We both knew that this time would come. I think I've always known it."

She looked up at him, her eyes shining. "Me, too."

He placed a soft kiss on her brow, another at her temple. Moving slowly, he reached behind her. But instead of loosening the hooks of her bra as she'd expected—no, wanted—him to do, he untied the scarf that was knotted at her nape.

His fingers brushed her neck, provoking another soft sound as he lifted the heavy fall of hair, tossed it in his hand and let the breeze separate the damp strands. Smiling slightly, he raised the scarf, a weightless banner of silk that stirred lightly in the air. "A token, my lady?" he asked.

Catriona sighed almost gratefully, then she smiled. His quaint invitation had slowed the swiftly expanding magic to a manageable pace. "Most certainly, m'lord," she responded with a touch of ceremony. "But you have no helmet."

A reckless smile curved his lips as he whipped the scarf into a rope and tied it around his head. It rode just above his brows like a sweatband. On anyone else the scarf would have looked ridiculous. On Beck MacDomhall, with his audacious smile, his tanned face and the wicked gleam in his eye, it gave him the look of a defiant pirate.

She altered the qualifying adjective—a defiant, *irresistible* pirate, who could very easily commandeer and plunder her emotions. Without much effort, he could steal something significant from her.

But she forgot that fact, just as she forgot to protest when he slid the satin straps off her shoulders and reached around her again. He fumbled slightly, an endearing sort of clumsiness.

She heard him catch his breath as her bra fell to the ground. She heard a soft invocation. His head bent, a shadow falling over his face.

And then there was no thinking at all for Catriona. Only feeling, a glorious, magnificent burst of feeling as his hands took the weight of her breasts and his mouth sought hers. His fingers brought her nipples to stunning life.

She was floating—in the air, across the heavens, on the wind—she didn't know where. She heard her name uttered hoarsely and unsteadily; she heard her own voice, whispering his name. Her heart soared; she felt free and light.

Bruising released the fragrance of the grasses, and she realized that somehow they were lying side by side on the curve of the berm.

The heat of his hands brought her down to earth, back to the breathtaking reality of passion, hot and hard and demanding. She made no protest when he removed her shorts. He stopped there, permitting her the small modesty of her panties. For now.

He loomed above her, his wide shoulders limned by the moonlight, his hands stroking her thighs, slowly, softly, until she thought she would weep if he didn't touch her. Even the scrap of her silk panties became unbearably restrictive.

Her hips rotated, picking up the rhythm of his caresses, silently pleading with him, using the movement of her body.

He leaned down and kissed the inside of her knee.

"Beck," she gasped, "please." Her hands skidded across his damp shoulders.

"What is it, my lady?" he murmured huskily, his breath warm and moist, higher on her thigh. "Tell me what you want."

She only just had the breath to answer. "You, I want you. Inside me."

He shuddered violently under her hands. His voice was thick as he cried, "Oh, Cat."

The silk was stripped from her and tossed aside. In seconds he was above her, poised for his possession. When he paused, she reached for him, her nails digging into the muscles of his hips.

He entered her slowly, easily, holding her cat-green gaze, his own gray eyes hooded and mysterious, until he filled her completely.

At last, when he felt her body's acceptance, he began to move, slowly at first, gradually faster, in a primitive, seductive rhythm, as old as time and as young as tomorrow. His thrusts were each deliberate and absolute, as though he would put his stamp of possession on her with each penetration.

She responded by lifting her hips to meet his demand, as though she too would make a claim on him and leave a mark of ownership. Slowly she slid her hands up his arms, over his damp skin, toward his neck. She felt his muscles tense, pulsating with his effort at control, as her fingers moved across his nape and into his hair. Blithely she refuted his effort, pulling him down until their mouths met and fused.

Like lightning, the precious control splintered to the winds. He moaned against her lips, her ear, her neck. His thrusts became raw and hungry, pushing her headlong to the precipice of fulfillment. She reached the edge, caught her breath and held it for an eternity, and then they were both falling, gasping, shuddering.

Softly, slowly, murmuring warm endearments, they came down to earth. Together. His breathing slowed, eased into a quiet, satiated heaviness against her breast. The honest aroma of pine and fertile earth blended with the honest, earthy smell of completion.

Keeping her in his arms, he rolled to his back. They lay there for a few moments, gazing up at the stars, letting the music lull their still-darting senses.

"This changes things, honey," he said pensively as he stroked her soft skin.

Cat sat up with a suddenness that took Beck by surprise.

His arm fell away, feeling oddly empty.

After a minute, she reached for her clothes and began to dress. Her movements were shaky.

"Yes," she said. "Yes, it does. I think I'll try to make the end of the concert after all. If I hurry I can change and get back before it's over."

"Cat..."

She put her hand on his arm. "Please, Beck, don't say anything more. Not right now."

He waited, but she didn't add anything else. Finally he got to his feet and pulled on his clothes. By the time they left the garden, walking close but not touching, he realized that a shadow had settled over their lovemaking, a shadow that might never go away.

Still waiting, still expecting some comment, some gesture to show him that the experience had meant as much to her as it had to him, he said good-night at her door.

Catriona closed the door behind her and leaned against it. She squeezed her eyes shut and released a piercing sigh. She had given up that significant part of herself to the irresistible pirate.

He had witnessed her submission, but did he know the extent of the commitment that went along with it?

If she was correct in her suspicions—no, she amended the thought, they were much more than suspicions; they were certainties. She recognized something that Beck seemed determined to deny. He had the same cognitive powers that Elena had. Maybe not as highly developed, not yet, but there. Definitely.

The one reason the people of Shared Ground would never give her quite the same degree of loyalty they gave to Elena was that she lacked that ability, that gift. She had tried to compensate by studying the law of the land in order to be as fair and impartial as possible, and the laws of Shared Ground in order to be prepared for the rare occasions when she'd be called on to arbitrate a dispute.

Beck might dismiss the MacDomhall powers as a carefully developed gift for observation or keen sense of hearing or whatever. But he had them. If she wasn't mistaken, they would get stronger.

So, if she was correct, then he was certainly aware of the depth of her feelings.

Where did that leave her?

Chapter 10

As dawn rose over the garden, Catriona sat at the window of her bedroom, letting the dew-laden breeze cool her face. She felt heavy all over—her arms, her legs, her heart. But at last she stirred herself.

It was a chore to wash, to brush her teeth, to dress. In place of breakfast, she forced one cup of coffee into her rebellious stomach; she needed the caffeine. Eating solid food was an impossibility.

She sensed that last night she and Beck had shared something that was unique and quite remarkable.

Something that was meant to be.

He'd said it first. He'd said that they both knew they were going to make love. Though neither of them had made a vow of forever, she'd felt the word there, hanging in the air between them. Maybe not completely ripened, maybe not fully matured, but ready to blossom.

Or was it? Was her interpretation of their relationship entirely different from his?

In the middle of their momentous lovemaking she had faced the temptation to tell Beck that she adored him, that if he wanted her, she would follow him wherever he went. Whenever and wherever he wanted her, needed her, she would be there.

She had faced the temptation and she had denied it. She thought she might die from the effort; it hurt in places deep inside that she'd never been aware of. But not until she'd gotten home had she finally given way to her tears and misery.

Throughout the night, she kept reminding herself over and over that she had a responsibility to the community. They couldn't both leave Shared Ground; they couldn't both walk out on Elena. He had given his word to return to Washington. That left her to step into Elena's shoes, to administer the community.

Four months ago that knowledge would have thrilled her. Her education, her training, her whole life had revolved around those plans.

But she also had obligations to herself, didn't she? The thought of never seeing Beck again—or seeing him only sporadically—was unbearable. What *was* she going to do?

Finally the moment arrived when she had to either face him or acknowledge her own spinelessness. She left her house and made her way along the path, past the fountain, past the statue, toward the greenhouses.

"It's going to be another scorcher," said Beck, wiping his brow. He made it a habit to be at the construction site every morning to check on the progress of the new greenhouse before he met Cat.

He and Brom Cunningham, one of the men on the crew, had become friendly. Brom was a quiet, wary man but they got along because Beck didn't ask any questions. He sensed the man didn't like questions.

This morning they were sitting on a huge roll of the unique paving material, sharing coffee from Brom's thermos and waiting for the foreman to arrive.

Brom nodded, then squinted up at the sky. "We might get some rain this afternoon, though," he said.

The garden was interesting, and working with Cat was more than pleasure, but Beck would really enjoy getting into the technological part of the community. This greenhouse for instance—the engineers had designed some kind of weather machine that sensed atmosphere and humidity and was programmed to respond to specific climate conditions instead of an arbitrary timer. This would be a subtropical climate, complete with temperature control, light manipulation, moisture from the soil and air.

Brom had confided that they were also working on the possibility of expanding the concept, on a limited basis, over open land.

Beck wanted to know more; he particularly wanted to know about the stone that rested so innocently among the rhododendrons. The community didn't have a geologist. He'd asked his grandmother about that, and her answer had been vague enough to be intriguing.

Besides, he reminded himself, he had a presidential directive to find out as much as he could while he was here.

He heard the crunch of footsteps on gravel and turned to see Cat on the path. He was worried about the way she'd left him so abruptly last night, but he couldn't tell a thing from her expression. He'd hoped her attitude might have sweetened this morning. He hoped she might be within reach.

"See you, Brom," he said absently, getting to his feet.

As he walked down the path to meet her, he changed his mind. It was ridiculously easy to read her emotional state, he thought with a sigh, and it sure as hell didn't take any kind of special powers to see that she had withdrawn from him even further.

He gave a rueful shake of his head as he walked along the path to meet her. "Good morning," he said as they drew abreast of each other. He smiled tenderly and started to grasp her shoulders, intending to draw her closer for a kiss.

Catriona answered the smile—it would have been impossible not to—but she resisted the physical contact. Gently she laid her hand on his chest.

He released his grip and shoved his hands into his jeans pockets instead. "Something the matter?" he asked casually.

She looked up at him. "Nothing an elimination of time and space wouldn't cure."

"That's a nice fantasy, but it's not all, is it?"

"No, that isn't all of it," she said evenly, stopping in the center of the path.

He faced her. He felt the beginnings of frustration. Right now he wished he *could* see into her mind.

He knew his perceptions were sharp. He'd always recognized and appreciated them, and the president had depended upon them. But with her, even those talents deserted him.

He would have to go with his feelings.

And his feelings were profound ones, he thought, looking down at her. Deep and tender emotions that were unfamiliar rose up within him. He knew without doubting that last night a bond had been formed between them, a spiritual joining, an attachment that would never be broken.

They turned and walked side by side to the section of the garden where they'd been working yesterday. He searched for words. When they reached the spot where they'd made love, he stopped her with a hand on her arm.

"Cat, no matter what happens, no matter how far apart we are physically, we'll always be together. I will never forget last night."

As they resumed their course, she reached for his hand but she didn't look at him. "I won't forget, either. I've gone over all the possibilities in my mind. I've thought about our having an affair for as long as you're here."

Just the memory of her naked in his arms accelerated his pulse, heated his blood and nourished his desire. His fingers tightened; there was a "but" in there someplace. Her head was bent forward, the blond hair shining in the sunlight. He couldn't see her face.

"But then I realized the danger in that, Beck. I'm afraid I don't have your strength. What might it do to me when you're gone for good?"

"I have no answer for you. I wish I did."

She nodded. "I know."

Using their entwined fingers, he stopped their progress. He cupped her chin with his free hand. She resisted but he made her look up. What he saw sent a sharp pain through him.

Her beautiful green eyes were the dull color of verdigris. Those eyes that should never know unhappiness were shimmering with moisture. "God, Cat." He realized that he'd never seen her cry, not even when she was a child. He'd seen other women cry, but not her. And he'd never had a woman's tears affect him like this.

She pushed at his hand, waved away his remorse. "Don't," she choked. "It isn't your fault. I'm sorry for crying." Her protest came out in short choppy phrases.

He couldn't think, his mind was a blur. He pulled her into his arms, his hands moved restlessly, comfortingly, over her back, but the comfort was for him, too. He spoke against her hair. "Let me try to explain. Please. I woke up this morning wondering if I had dreamed what happened here." He gestured, indicating the scene without looking at it, then he returned his hand to her back, spreading his fingers wide to hold as much of her as he could.

"But I knew I hadn't dreamed it. No dream could ever be vivid enough to reflect the truth of what we shared here. We had something extraordinary and vital. If, God forbid, we never made love to each other again, I would still never feel completely alone as long as I have the memory of last night."

She had pulled back to look up into his face. Now she watched him with a stunned expression. She still didn't understand.

He cradled her face with both his hands and went on, almost desperately, "I know with a certainty I can't explain that no matter how far apart we are, no matter how many years, how many miles separate us, that we will always be drawn back to one another. I know that, Cat. I want you to know it, too."

Cat reached up to touch his cheek. A sorrowful smile curved her lips. He could barely look at her eyes.

"Don't you see?" she said softly, so softly that he had to bend his head to hear her. "That is my greatest fear. You've put it quite beautifully, quite succinctly."

Suddenly he understood. And if he'd thought he felt guilt and pain at the sight of her tears, it was nothing to what he felt now.

You damned arrogant fool.

He had done her the gravest injustice of all when he'd admitted how special their lovemaking was. He knew how she thought. He didn't think that way but, as far as there being some supernatural connection, she'd lived too long in Shared Ground where people tended to believe in that sort of thing.

It would have been better for her, for him, if he'd treated it casually. Her feelings were deep. She would have hurt but she would have recovered, deciding some day in the future that he was a selfish bastard and not worth her grief.

As it was, at the end of a year he would leave and this woman would wait here, caught like a prisoner in a trap. "Cat?"

Her eyes never left his face. "Yes?"

He put his hand over hers, holding her warm fingers in place against his cheek. "Time and space, that was what you said you needed."

She nodded.

"I'll give them to you. It will be hard as hell, but I'd give you anything in my power to give."

The rest of the day was miserable. Each time they touched, they jerked apart as though they'd been stung. Catriona looked up more than once to find his hungry gaze on her. And she caught herself doing the same thing, her eyes lingering wishfully on him.

It was almost funny. Almost. By the time they parted they were being terribly polite to each other.

The other thing that was on her mind—she couldn't talk about that yet. Not after last night. She was going to have to think about it for a few days.

Catriona dreaded the next day. She knew in her heart that Beck was deeply troubled. She also knew that he was frustrated. She recognized the condition because she was frustrated, too. The night had been interminably long.

But she resolved to protect herself.

He had too much of her.

Beck was already at work. "Come in here, Cat," he said decisively as he hefted a tray of pine seedlings they had planned to set out on the brow of the mountain today. "I've got to talk to you."

She was startled by the brusque tone. It wasn't what she expected. She searched his tight expression and saw concern there, and anger. "Beck, I know what you're going to say."

He set the tray beside the door to be moved out later and turned back to her. "You do?"

"Yes." She sat down on a bench and laced her fingers together. "You would like for us to make love again."

He slid his hands into the back pockets of his jeans and stood there looking down at her. "Well, yeah, there's that," he said.

"And you think I'm being difficult." She tilted her head back to look up at him and resisted the urge to pace. He'd already recognized that she paced only when she was confronted with a problem. This morning she had to remain calm, rational. "You realize, of course, that I can never leave Shared Ground. And you understand that I have to protect myself."

She wondered if he read more into her statement than she wanted him to know. She wondered if he knew that she was falling in love with him.

"You're a prisoner here," he stated.

"I'm *not* a prisoner."

"You consider yourself answerable for the success of this whole community. The prison may be self-imposed but it's a prison, nonetheless." He seemed to realize that he had raised his voice, and he took a breath. When he spoke again he used a more reasonable tone. "One person can't be accountable, Cat. One person just can't do it."

"But I'm also accountable to myself. Certainly, one person can't do everything. It takes the cooperation of everyone," Catriona answered heatedly.

She jumped up, paced a few steps and whirled on him, unable to control her agitation any longer. "Much as I would like to, I can't just walk away from my responsibilities." She punctuated the statement with a wave of her hand.

Then she realized what she'd said.

His mouth curved in amusement. "Much as you would like to?" he quoted into the stillness that had fallen on her words.

That was what happened when you didn't watch what you said, she thought disgustedly. "A figure of speech," she said, with what she hoped was credence. "We can't both leave here, Beck. This garden is irreplaceable, and not just to the community. You, of all people, should realize that it would be like pouring a treasure down the sewer. What would happen to the community? To Elena?"

At once the amusement was wiped from his face. He turned away, and again she was struck by the feeling that something else was on his mind. Something unrelated to this conversation.

He raked a hand through his hair and stood staring at the ground. "The same thing that happens to other small towns. It might suffer but it would survive," he said in an infinitely sad, quiet voice. He seemed to be talking more to himself than her. "God, I hope it would survive," he added in a whisper.

Catriona returned to his side. Clearly there was more to this than their relationship, more than she understood. "Beck, what is it? I know you appreciate the progress we've made in Shared Ground as much as anybody. Why would you say such a thing?"

"I don't know. Just this . . . itchy feeling I've got," he admitted. "Cat, I know you're still afraid I'm going to take this job away from you."

Am I? she asked herself. *Or am I afraid you won't?*

He sighed and ran his fingers through his hair. His hand lingered at the back of his neck, stretching his shirt over the muscles of his chest. "I don't know what to say to convince you that I'm not. I gave the president my word to return at the end of the year. Even if I hadn't— and I'm not indispensable—it would take him a long time to replace me.

"It's our history together, don't you see? When he needs someone to hash something over, he can toss out ideas, without having to worry about how wild they are. And he doesn't have to stop and explain why he feels a certain way, which he would have to do with a new man.

"Even if I decided that I wanted to walk away from my job with the president, I couldn't do it."

Catriona wondered if he realized that he was quoting her earlier admission, almost word for word. Probably not. But her heart gave a little leap.

Chapter 11

Beck and Catriona parted at the statue of John MacDomhall, he to return to his grandmother's cottage where, as she did during most of their lunch meals, Elena would instruct him.

Catriona went off down the path toward her own house. Beck watched her go, concerned. There was a deliberate spring in her step, too deliberate. It hurt him to watch her. When he touched her, she stiffened, so he stopped touching her. That hurt worse.

It had been a week since they made love. A week of frustration, and a week of attempting to walk in a field of eggshells without breaking one.

He sensed that Cat was like a wire strung to its absolute limit. One wrong move and it would pop. The resulting backlash could do major damage. So he walked on eggshells.

He looked at the garden around him, breathed in the fresh scents of humus, of soil and sprouting plants. But the peace he was beginning to know, to depend on, eluded him.

Was he in love with Cat? He wasn't sure what love was, but his feelings were powerful.

Was she in love with him? With his words, he'd crippled her, chained her to feelings that he could do nothing about.

Nothing. Not a damned thing. He couldn't stay here. He couldn't take her with him.

He was going to abandon her, just as her mother had abandoned her, leaving her alone. He felt like the champion selfish bastard. He'd been calling himself that for a week. His thoughts still churning, he stalked toward Elena's house.

He was supposed to be the wunderkind, supposed to be able to sense trouble before it started, head it off; but Cat had seen the danger before he had. His only thoughts had been about the thrill and magnitude of the thing that had happened between them.

He certainly wasn't a celibate; there had been women through the years. When he was in his late twenties and still too full of youthful juices, he'd been more than willing to accommodate the women who were drawn like sticky-footed flies to the ultimate seduction—power. But it hadn't taken him long to recognize the emptiness, the lack of fulfillment. Later there had been affairs, genuine but still lacking something vital.

Yet there had never been anything even approaching the emotion he'd experienced making love with Cat. Hell, he'd never even used that word—lovemaking—preferring instead the nomenclature of the times—relationship, affair, intimate friendship.

He gave a bark of laughter at the last; it belittled the word *friend,* making it somehow less than it was. And it did the same to the word, *intimate,* which implied more than the physical.

She would never leave here and he couldn't blame her for that. There was something in Shared Ground that redeemed the spirit, nourished the soul and made for happiness. He was almost tempted . . . No, that was impossible. But he could see his feelings reflected in the faces of the people here.

Hell, MacDomhall, you're turning into a damned armchair philosopher.

Catriona felt Beck's eyes boring into her back as she left him standing at the statue.

Her movements were automatic. She entered her house through the kitchen, then she fixed her lunch. She made a salad and poured a tall glass of iced tea and sat at the table on the patio. She had taken only a bite or two when she heard her family of local robins playing around the chestnut tree. The babies had learned to fly. Soon they would be gone.

She pushed her plate aside, closed her eyes and dropped her forehead onto her folded arms. A stifled sob broke from her throat. She had never felt so alone in her life.

Beck had been puzzled by her quiet demeanor this morning. She'd caught the questioning looks he'd thrown at her as they worked in the greenhouse, but how on earth could she explain?

Maybe Elena could make him understand.

Darn it. Where was his ESP when she needed it?

Elena had confirmed what Catriona had observed over the past weeks on her own.

His mind was amazing; he seemed to drink in knowledge like a dry, thirsty plant. Only rarely did he require assimilation time, time to absorb and process the information they were pouring into him. Once in a while he would pause, walk away, hands deep in his pockets, head bent, to analyze something he'd been told. The pause was always brief. But the other matter...

She was brought out of her reverie by the sound of the two young robins squabbling on one of the lower branches of the tree. With a small smile, she lifted her head to watch. After a minute, the birds scattered into the air, into other trees, off to attend to other business.

That was what she should be doing, attending to business. She sighed, rose and took her plate and glass to the kitchen.

Determinedly she put aside her dejected mood. She had a lot to do. She would waste no more time on regret.

Her ambition had not ebbed. She still wanted to be the Gardener, she wanted the position of leadership she'd trained for, but she was beginning to have a clearer vision of her responsibility to the community as a whole. She could see that the good of Shared Ground would be best served with Beck as its leader.

Though he still maintained that he wouldn't stay in Tennessee, she could see the value of his presence and the tremendous contribution he could make if he could be convinced to remain here permanently.

Whatever developed, she wasn't inclined to bow out of the race completely. She wanted to be a part of that "whatever." But if he stayed, that would put her into the back seat. Would she be content to stay there?

After lunch Beck found Catriona in the lab, working on the nutrient enrichment studies. Silently he joined her at the bench and reached for the file on the experiment.

She risked a glance at his strong profile. He seemed preoccupied. He flipped his medallion from finger to finger, across his knuckles. The action was smooth and practiced and told her more than words could that he often tinkered with it like this.

"I've always carried it," he said absently, as though she'd asked.

The afternoon dragged on and Catriona's mood didn't improve. She knew exactly what was wrong with her. She'd never been able to settle down when there was a formidable task to be performed.

At last she reached a decision. Or, to be honest with herself, she acknowledged the decision she'd reached hours earlier. Maybe the decision had never been hers to make, but the subject was one which she, and she alone, could introduce.

"Beck, I think we need to talk," she said as they finished for the day.

"About what?"

She shrugged and smiled, hoping that she looked composed. "Business things."

He gave her a sharp look. "Shall I come over to your place after dinner?" he asked huskily. His gray eyes were dark, and she saw the heat in their smoky depths.

"No," she answered too quickly. She was in real danger of laughing hysterically. He was on the wrong track this time, and he would be furious when he found out what she really wanted to talk about.

"Let me join you at Elena's after dinner instead. She will need to hear what I have to say."

When Beck left Washington, knowing that he wouldn't return for a year, there had been more to his uneasiness than he could explain to himself, more than simply a year away from his job. Those additional res-

ervations, which had been vague up until now, suddenly took substantive form. The itchy feeling he'd had
for a week had grown stronger every day, and now it was
full blown.

Something was going on in that clever mind, he realized, staring at her. Something that didn't have a thing
to do with them. And he had a feeling he wasn't going
to like it worth a damn.

"Fine," he said guardedly.

That evening when Catriona arrived, she found Beck
and Elena sitting beneath the ginkgo tree, talking quietly. Over their heads the branches of the graceful tree
stirred lightly in the breeze.

The ginkgo was one of the first trees to assume its autumn color. Even now, she could see that a few of the
fan-shaped leaves were beginning to show traces of yel-
low. In another couple of weeks the tree would be completely transformed from its light summer green to the
characteristic brilliance of vivid gold. The scene was a
forcible reminder that the weeks and months were passing. Well, if she was successful tonight, time wouldn't
matter.

The soft illumination of fading twilight was aug-
mented by a light from inside Elena's study. In minutes
it would be dark.

Beck rose, ducking under a branch, as she approached. He touched her and she pulled away quickly,
too quickly. He didn't miss the withdrawal. A muscle in
his jaw twitched in reaction. But she had to keep her
distance. She *had* to.

"Good evening, Catriona," said Elena serenely.

"Good evening," she answered. She was both exhilarated and disturbed by the coming struggle, because she had no doubt—a struggle it would be.

She had dressed for it, taking care with her appearance. Her hair was piled loosely at the crown of her head. The creamy white skirt was full and graceful, and the matching ruffled peasant-style blouse was very feminine. She wiped her hands in the fold of her skirt.

Beck caught her at it. His gaze held hers, but his eyes gave nothing away. She couldn't tell whether he was amused or annoyed by the outward sign of nervousness, and she wondered if he read what she was going to say. She was certain that Elena did.

"There seems to be a nip in the air tonight," said Elena, breaking into their silent exchange.

Catriona and Beck turned simultaneously. They both started to speak at once, but Beck won out. "Would you like to go inside, Elena?"

She gave him a speaking look. "It isn't *that* cold," she said testily. "I wish you two wouldn't treat me like an old woman." She realized what she'd said and laughed at herself. "But I think I would like a nice cup of tea. How about you, Catriona?"

Beck made a move toward the house, but Catriona spoke first. "I'll get it." She was grateful for the tiny delay. She entered the kitchen and moved instinctively but deliberately, heating water, taking cups and saucers from the cabinet, filling the pot with tea, slicing a lemon.

When she returned with the tray, she noticed that Beck had brought another chair, but she shook her head. "No thanks." She passed the tray to them and then sat on the grass beside Elena's chair.

Beck looked at both women for a minute and then took up a stance against the tree. He folded his arms across his broad chest and waited.

Catriona dropped her eyes under his dark, hot gaze and set her cup aside. She pulled idly at the grass in front of her. "I wanted to talk to you both because I've discovered a few things that have made me rethink our situation here. Perhaps it isn't my place to raise the issue..." She deliberately let her voice trail off and looked to Elena, who shook her head.

"Go ahead, Catriona," said the older woman.

She dropped the shredded grass and dusted off her fingers. "Having Beck here in Shared Ground has changed my—the situation—drastically." She paused, giving them time and opportunity for interruption. In a way, she wished Elena *would* take over.

Grandson and grandmother, however, were silent, waiting for her to continue. Elena's expression was knowing; Beck's was clouded.

"First, Beck is truly a quick study." She gave him a swift glance and a brief smile. "I'm not a cynic but I did have some reservations about your learning what you needed to know in one year. I assumed you were intelligent, Beck, but, I have to admit, I'm flabbergasted by your capacity."

She realized she was talking too fast, almost chattering, and she stopped for breath. "Second, and most important, we all should concede right up front that there are some things I will never be able to do as Gardener."

Elena did interrupt then, the lines in her face diminished by her bittersweet smile. "But you have trained yourself well, my dear. I know what you're about to say."

At that Beck looked at them both, his distrust plain on his face. "What's this ab—"

Elena ignored him. "Before you go on, Catriona, I want you to know that I have no qualms about leaving Shared Ground in your hands, should it be necessary."

"But it isn't necessary." She turned her eyes to Beck in mute appeal, hoping, praying that he wouldn't take this as a betrayal. "Beck, you have the aptitude that I lack. You can fight it till doomsday, you can deny it forever, but it *is* there. And you need to develop it while you have Elena to help you."

He had been motionless through the last part of her speech, but a small blaze had ignited far back in his eyes. Suddenly he straightened from his comfortable slouch. He stepped away from the tree, towering over her. His broad shoulders seemed massive, and the blaze in his eyes had become a fire storm. His expression was unyielding and inflexible and worse, it closed her out, totally and completely.

No! Beck wanted to shout, to roar. *No! You're wrong.* "Don't say it, Cat," he warned instead, in a voice that was like death. "You know I don't believe in these phenomenal extrasensory powers you two are so fixed on."

But you *do.* She clasped her fingers together in her lap and looked at him, trying desperately to communicate through this medium that she didn't understand.

He ignored her silent plea and continued, "Elena has just said she has complete trust in your leadership. And that's good enough for me. I've already told both of you why it's impossible for me to remain here after the year is over." His torment, hidden away from her somewhere behind his eyes, was finally revealed in his voice. "You said you understood."

She didn't have to be able to read minds to grasp his meaning. There was accusation in his voice as well. Presumably he was speaking to both of them, but the words were directed at Catriona and she knew it.

She fought a silent battle with herself. God knows, she wasn't trying to add guilt concerning her to his other burdens, she wasn't using their lovemaking as a weapon.

But she could see that he would take it that way. How could she convince him of that while still pleading the case for what she knew was right?

Suddenly the words came to her. Fed by Elena? Or by Beck himself? Or had they been there all along, deep in her own subconscious?

"I do understand, Beck," she told him very quietly, very sincerely. "It isn't so much that Shared Ground needs you, though it's true that you would be an invaluable addition to this community." She broke off, looking at Elena, but there would be no help there, not at this time anyway.

She returned her gaze to his and held it there by the sheer force of her determination. Her heart was racing like a runaway freight train, but she refused to yield to the temptation to look away. Urgently, unwaveringly she willed him to listen, to read her thoughts, to do whatever it took to trust her.

"Beck," she said finally, her voice low with the effort. "The need, I believe, is yours. I think you've found something here that has been missing from your life for a long, long time." He made some move, shifting his body as though he would protest. She shook her head to ward off the intended interruption. "No, not me. Something here in the mountains, in the community. I think you need Shared Ground every bit as much, if not more, than we need you," she finished firmly, boldly.

Silence, a silence so dense and heavy she could almost feel it, settled on her shoulders like a dark, dusky mantle. She held her breath, waiting for his response.

Outraged, his gaze narrowed in fury, Beck stared at her. His fists clenched until she could see the veins stand out in his arms. There was something wild behind his eyes, like a caged animal desperate for freedom. She closed her eyes under the onslaught, then opened them again.

Without warning, he broke the visual contact. He spun on his heel and disappeared beyond the small pool of illumination, into the night.

Catriona let the air escape from her lungs; her shoulders slumped. She felt like a deflated balloon.

Elena's face remained inscrutable, but finally she bowed her head. Some of her energy seemed to have drained away, too. They heard his footfalls, purposeful and precipitant on the gravel road, growing fainter with distance as he strode away.

Catriona's heart was squeezed by regret, as though she had betrayed him by speaking. She knew exactly where he was going. Into the forest. Up the mountain. To the belvedere.

She made a move to rise, to follow, but Elena stopped her with a hand on her shoulder. "Not now," she said. "Leave him be."

"Maybe I can—"

Elena shook her head. "He feels trapped."

"I know."

"I coerced him into what he feels is exile," Elena said with a poignant smile. "I used his concern for—and loyalty to—a man whom he venerates to force him to return here." She looked away for a minute, into the darkness. "Perhaps it was a mistake, perhaps I asked too much."

"You asked for a small segment of his life," Catriona protested. "How can that be too much?"

"But you asked for more. You suggested permanence."

There was no accusation in Elena's statement. She was merely reiterating a fact, but Catriona slewed her gaze away. "I'm—"

"Sorry? Don't be. It had to be brought into the open, you know. He gave me his word to remain for a year, and he gave his word to the president that he would return at the end of that time. Only now, I'm afraid, he sees the truth of your observation. Or maybe he saw it long ago, maybe that is why he's fought so hard. He is in terrible pain, Catriona." That same pain was reflected clearly in her own eyes.

Catriona reached for her hand.

"He is torn between his duty to his mentor and his newfound sense of what is right for himself," Elena went on. "And for you."

Catriona was perfectly aware that Elena could see through any pretense she might make. Thank goodness, the older woman didn't proceed with the subject of her personal involvement.

"I was afraid a year wouldn't be enough time." Elena sighed heavily, her fragile, aged form shuddering with the effort. "Now you've made him see how difficult it will be for him to leave when that time is over."

Catriona let her head droop onto their clasped hands. "But he *will* leave," she said, her voice merely a thin thread of sound. "He will return to Washington. He gave his word."

Elena didn't respond. There was nothing more to be said.

Catriona allowed herself a few moments of hopeless fantasy imagining a happy ending. She and Beck living together in Shared Ground, carrying on the work of his ancestors, loving, raising a family.

But real life didn't work that way. In real life, happy endings were rare. And, perhaps, too, a happy ending from her point of view wouldn't turn out so happily for Beck.

She sighed and got to her feet. "Good night, Elena."

Beck stood at the wall of the belvedere and looked out over the valley. Clouds obscured the moon and a light rain had begun to fall. He plunged his hands through his hair and massaged the tight muscles at the back of his neck.

Damn! What the hell was he going to do?

He'd been furious when he left Elena and Cat. Now he was just tired, bone tired. He'd trudged for hours and ended up here. It must be close to midnight.

He sighed and leaned one hip against the wall, looking down into the dark abyss below. For the first time in his thirty-four years, he was having a confrontation with his own regret, regret that his life hadn't followed the path tradition had set down for him.

A melancholy expression crossed his face as he contemplated what it would have been like—a peaceful life of harmony with the natural world, a life of contemplation, study and reflection. He would never have known the stress, the frustration, the disillusionment that were by-products of reality in the outside world. But neither would he have known the excitement, the action, the sense of achievement. That was the life for him, he thrived on the chaos of his job. He would never be content here.

Often the present was a difficult time to be alive. He dropped his hands and shook his head with a rueful smile. It was also thrilling and awesome, with technological advances sprouting, budding—blooming as fast as the herbs and flowers in Catriona's garden.

Catriona. He sighed again and began the long walk back to the cottage.

The telephone rang downstairs.

The president was the one who insisted he have a phone installed in his grandmother's house in case of emergency. Elena had grudgingly agreed, but she refused to use it.

With a frown he looked at the clock. Two in the morning. Suddenly his heart plunged to his gut. No one else would be calling, not at this hour.

He yanked on his jeans; he was out the door and on the stairs when he heard Elena's voice. "Yes, he's here. Just a moment, please." She turned, holding out the receiver.

When he took it from her, she stopped only long enough to give him a reassuring touch on the arm. Then she returned to her room and closed the door behind her.

"MacDomhall," he barked harshly.

"Beck, I'm afraid we have a problem," said the president.

Chapter 12

Catriona was awakened at two-thirty by a pounding on her door. Whatever it was about couldn't be good news. Not at this hour. She reached for her robe and hurried to the stairs, slipping her arms in as she went. She didn't stop to tie the belt but flung open the door.

Beck was standing there.

She caught her breath, unsure what to expect. Her hand tightened on the knob. "Beck? Is something wrong?"

His dark eyes reflected grief. "I'm afraid I have some bad news."

Her gaze widened in horror. "Has something happened to Elena?"

He reached out to touch her shoulder, smoothed a strand of hair from her face. "God, no, honey. I'm sorry. I didn't mean—" He broke off. "Elena's fine."

Suddenly she realized his attention was absorbed, distracted. His gaze roamed over her tangled hair, dropped to her breasts, clearly visible between the lapels of her open robe. He smiled slightly. "You look mighty appealing when you're right out of bed. Very sexy," he said in a soft, warm drawl.

She blushed, pushed her hair back and pulled the sides of her robe together. She had some trouble finding the ends of the belt, but finally her clumsy fingers managed the task. "Come in," she said.

He recovered himself, stepped over the threshold. "Cat, we're going to have to put aside our differences for a while. I have a serious problem and I need your help."

"Are you leaving?" she asked bluntly. *Have I driven you away?* she added to herself.

He looked puzzled for a minute, then he smiled and skimmed her cheek with the back of his knuckles. He couldn't seem to keep from touching her. She didn't object; his touch was somehow reassuring.

"No, Cat. At least not...I may have to go for a while. But you aren't the reason, honey."

"You were angry."

He nodded. "I was furious." He studied her face. "You didn't think I'd leave without saying a word?"

She didn't know what she thought. "Well, I didn't expect to see you. Not until—" *Not until you'd had time to cool off.* "Not tonight."

She closed the door behind him and led the way into the living room. She snapped on a lamp and took the chair beside the fireplace. "Have a seat."

He sat in the chair opposite her. "No, it's something else completely. This is about the garden, the secret compound. The president called a short time ago. It seems that one of his staff was very suspicious of his sudden recovery and my part in it. The man's name is

Roger Henderson and he has sent someone—a snoop, a spy—to infiltrate Shared Ground.''

Stunned, Catriona leaned against the back of her chair. "Tell me," she said faintly.

So he told her, leaving out nothing.

The president had informed Beck that Roger Henderson had overheard their conversation at Camp David. He'd been dropping hints for several days, and finally the president had called him in for a conference. When confronted, Henderson had confessed he'd eavesdropped. He'd also admitted sending a spy to Tennessee to find out what was going on in Beck MacDomhall's hometown.

"Henderson seemed certain that I would be pleased. I'm afraid I overreacted, Beck," the president had said. "I was so furious that I fired the son of a bitch on the spot. A few minutes later I realized my mistake— I should have found out exactly how much was speculation and suspicion and how much was real knowledge. I called the gate to stop him from leaving, but I was too late. Now he has disappeared."

As he had listened, Beck had felt his stomach hit his feet. He had been the one to divulge the full secret, the only one—ever—in the history of Shared Ground.

Good God! If knowledge leaked that a secret alkaloid compound, a miracle drug, had saved the president's life, the community would be doomed.

A man who knew the secret would show no mercy where such knowledge and its potential financial rewards were at stake. Geographical isolation wouldn't serve. The world would descend on this quiet, peaceful place and turn it into a circus.

When he reached that point in the story, Cat came to kneel in front of him. She slid her hands along his shoulders, into the hair at his nape.

At first Beck's guilt made him resist the comfort she was offering, but then he pulled her up into his arms and onto his lap and held her close against his chest, thankful for her warm presence, her understanding.

He took one hand in his, pressing a kiss into the palm, then wrapped his arms around her, as though to absorb her sweetness, her strength.

Suddenly his stony countenance twisted with guilt. "God, Cat. What have I done?" he groaned, burying his face in her hair.

Catriona curled against him. His heart thundered under her cheek. She'd never thought to witness this concern for the future of the community in him.

His hands moved restlessly, absently, over her arms, her back, and she felt his spine adjust as though the tactile sensation somehow reinforced his determination. When he resumed the narrative, she tilted her head back to observe his face.

She could almost see the wheels begin to turn, feel the determination flowing back into his body.

"The only other information he was able to give me was that Henderson's infiltrator was under orders not to make contact until the mission is complete."

"Isn't that unusual?"

He shook his head. "Not necessarily. Obviously Henderson heard enough to understand that Shared Ground is isolated. He probably figured regular reporting would be difficult. He didn't want the man to blow his cover. It has to be someone I don't know, of course."

He was thinking aloud, ideas delivered randomly, as he stared at a point over his head. His mind seemed to race ahead of his words as he explained the situation to her. He was planning, pulling ideas from deep in his brain, examining them, discarding some, cataloging others for further study. He was also drawing on her warmth, her strength.

"The president has offered us any help we might need to identify him, but anything we do—like call in the FBI to locate Henderson—will only compound the problem by raising more questions."

She understood the frustration that she heard in his voice. He was accustomed to the unrestricted use of such resources. Now they were closed to him.

She also understood something he'd said to her months ago when they were in Washington. He'd cautioned her about the inevitability of disclosure, and she'd dismissed his warning too carelessly. Now her mind spun ahead, too, seeking a solution. If disclosure was inevitable, could it be contained or directed in some way?

"Don't punish yourself, Beck." She reached up to touch his whiskered cheek. The day's growth of beard gave him a rakish look and scratched against her fingertips. "You had no choice but to explain to the president. Good Lord, you'd just given the man his health back. He was bound to question you. Had he been a different kind of person, he might have even had you detained."

He ducked his chin to smile down at her. But the smile still carried a load of guilt. "If he'd been a different kind of person, this whole situation would have been moot. As it is, I've revealed the secret, something that has not happened for almost three hundred years."

"Stop that," she said. Agitated, she squirmed free of his arms and stood. She began to pace. "I would have explained, too, had I been in your shoes. You have to forget guilt, Beck," she said. "We need your strength more, and we certainly need your expertise."

"You're right," he said after a pause. "What's done can't be changed. Now we have to think of a way to handle it."

She went back to her chair. "Good. Let's study this carefully, Beck. There may be a chance that we can locate the man ourselves. I do know that only three people have been accepted into the community since you arrived," she offered.

He raised his head. His eyes were on her face, but his attention was focused elsewhere. "Yes," he murmured. "The president can run a check on three people without raising too many eyebrows."

Suddenly she thought of another unpleasant topic that had to be broached. "Do we tell Elena?"

She had his attention again. He sighed and muttered a curse. "No. I sneaked out of the house like a truant after the call. We may have to tell her later, but I'd rather take a shot at solving this without worrying her."

"Of course she'll know without being told."

"Maybe." His expression was noncommittal.

She shook her head and smiled for the first time since he'd arrived. "When will you learn that you don't put anything over on Elena?" She sighed. "But I agree that we should try. What can I do?"

"We need some background information about these three men. Does Elena keep any sort of records on the people who join the community?"

"No."

He was surprised. "Nothing? No information at all?"

She shook her head. "No, and I should tell you that none of them were recruited. They all came to us off the hiking trails."

He knew that this often happened during the summer, when the trails were heavily used. People stumbled onto the small community. If the Gardener approved, some stayed on. "That makes our job a lot harder," he said wryly. "God, I wish I knew which one was the spy." He thought for a minute then he moved his shoulders as though to relieve them of an unnecessary burden. "Okay," he added decisively. "What *do* we know?"

Catriona had begun to pace again, the long, full skirt of her robe billowing about her ankles when she turned. "We know their names. Will Heath, Bromley Cunningham, John Castleberry." She ticked them off.

"I didn't realize Brom had arrived after I did." He frowned, then collected himself. "We will need more than names to give the president. We need to know where they are from, where they went to school, if they served in the military." Once more he frowned and returned to the subject of Brom Cunningham. "I've gotten to know Brom pretty well and I like him. I'd hate to think it was him, but he doesn't open up about himself."

"Brom has been quiet ever since he arrived, but that isn't so unusual." She hesitated. "It wouldn't be the first time that someone has come to Shared Ground needing to heal, Beck."

"I know." He shook his head. "And I can't believe he's the one. Who are the others?"

"Will is an engineer, too, and he's working at the rec center." The community was in the process of expanding the recreational facilities.

"John is another example of someone who needs to heal. His wife died last year. He's in the office with our dentist, Dr. Robertson, who's ready to retire. We were lucky that John showed up when he did."

Suspicion gleamed in his eyes. "Coincidence?"

She shrugged. "I don't know. But I should think it would be hard to fake training as a dentist. And I'm sure Dr. Robertson checked his credentials."

Beck stood up, his hopes beginning to rise. He was glad to be moving on this, to have a plan, to be doing *something*. "In the morning I'll talk to Brom. Then I'll go to the center and talk to Will." He grinned. "You can have the dentist."

"Me?" Catriona touched her jaw defensively. Like all of the native residents of Shared Ground who benefited from a lifelong plan of oral hygiene, she never had problems with her teeth. Except for her yearly checkup, she didn't even go to the dentist. "I don't have an appointment," she said with a grimace.

He laughed briefly, but almost immediately he was serious again. "We have no time to waste, Cat. You'll think of something."

She met his eyes, agreeing with the need for speed. "I'll think of something," she repeated.

"Well, I'd better be going." He paused beside her. "This probably could have waited until morning," he admitted.

No, she thought, looking at the lines of worry that still scored his face. He had needed her. She didn't know why that meant so much, but it did. "I'm glad you came to me tonight."

"I'll take off and let you get a couple of hours of sleep." He dipped his head and covered her mouth with a soft, hungry kiss.

She was ready to cast her reservations aside; she was about to respond, when he swung around abruptly and headed for the door. She followed more slowly. She thought about asking him to stay, but, in the end, she didn't.

"Let's go into town and see what information we can get out of them," said Beck.

They were walking in the garden. His arm was around her waist. A few minutes ago, when he'd put it there, his touch had sent heat down her spine. She'd started to draw away in self-defense, but she'd stopped herself and now she'd begun to relax.

"We'll meet back at your place before lunch." He gave her an absentminded kiss.

"Okay," she said to his retreating back.

He must have heard the dissatisfaction in her voice, because he swung back immediately. With a grin, he lifted her off her feet and this kiss was completely effective.

Catriona smiled as she watched him walk out of sight, unable to explain this lighthearted mood, especially in view of the threat they faced. She thought for a moment. She certainly wasn't going to feign a toothache.

As a matter of fact, she *had* a good excuse. Before Beck arrived, she had been working on a natural compound to replace the chemical fluoride-type treatment that Dr. Robertson had been using on the children's teeth. It wasn't ready, but she could discuss it with him, come up with a question or two and then steer the conversation to the new dentist. That would have to do as a pretext, because Dr. Robertson would see right through her if she tried anything silly, like a toothache.

She had to search for her notes; she finally located them and started off, hoping he wasn't going to inquire as to why she was bringing along the same notes they'd discussed the last time she was in his office. When she arrived in town, she found that fabrication wouldn't be necessary.

"Dr. Robertson has gone fishing," John Castleberry told her, his welcoming smile white in sharp contrast against his black skin.

She sincerely hoped the intruder wasn't John. She liked him. He was a nice man, quiet spoken, middle-aged. A widower. Or so he'd said when he arrived. She explained her reason for the visit.

"Come in, Catriona. I was just going over some of his case histories. Tell me more about the compound."

So she spent a pleasant morning with John Castleberry. He was from Wilkes-Barre, Pennsylvania. He and his wife had been childless and he couldn't be happier, or more grateful, that he'd been accepted in Shared Ground, which he'd stumbled on while hiking in the mountains. "I never dreamed there was a place like this on earth," said John, with moisture in his eyes and a soft longing in his voice. "I only wished Jean had lived to see it. She would have loved Shared Ground. Particularly the garden. She was quite a . . ." His voice trailed off.

Catriona touched his hand, hating the deception she'd had to practice for this man whom she'd grown fond of. "I wish so, too, John. I would have liked to have known her. We are very grateful that you found us."

She remembered her first sight of him two months ago in Elena's cottage. He had been so lonely, so thin and gray, his face lined with suffering. Now he had gained a bit of weight; his expression, though still harboring traces of grief, revealed a warm, loving man who was beginning to hope for a better life. The intruder couldn't be John.

Beck wasn't faring much better than Catriona. He had talked to both the men and found himself hoping that neither of them was the intruder. Will Heath was a fair and brawny man, open and friendly, not the type to hide under a clandestine identity.

Brom Cunningham was more puzzling. He didn't volunteer any information. A quiet, dark-haired giant, Brom was an efficient and imaginative engineer. But he was frequently withdrawn, almost sullen. Beck was treated to a burst of his hot temper, too, when Brom finally realized that he was being persistently, if subtly, interrogated.

"Have you got a gripe or a complaint against me, MacDomhall?" he demanded. "If you have, why don't you spit it out?"

Beck had no intention of being put on the defensive with this man. He didn't answer. Instead he studied him calmly, assessing the outburst. There was some florid color in his face, but that could be the result of anger. "Should I have, Brom?"

Briefly and succinctly, Cunningham told Beck where he could put his complaint, turned on his heel and stalked away.

Beck was much too discerning to base his suspicions on the basis of surface appearance—con artists were inevitably likable, and a man with an open, up-front personality could be hiding the darkest secrets. But in this case, he leaned reluctantly toward the obvious suspect—Brom Cunningham.

He was leaving the greenhouse construction site when he spotted Cat. "Hey!" he called, and quickened his step to catch up. When he reached her side, he put his arm across her shoulders and slowed his pace to match her shorter stride. "Anything?" he inquired quietly.

She repeated the personal information she'd pried out of John, and Beck briefed her on his own observations.

"I hate this, Beck," she admitted when he'd finished.

"Yeah. Me, too." He slid one hand under the fall of her hair, cupping her nape. They walked on. "The hell of it is, Cat, I admire both of those men. Brom is sullen and detached, but there may be a perfectly good reason for the way he acts. He's plenty smart."

"Maybe we should go to Elena. After all, she's the one who made the judgment to include these men in the community. I don't like to feel that we're usurping her authority."

"We may have to talk to her, but she's not going to like our interference." The responsibility for his grandmother's reaction—be it anger or disillusionment—was his.

He could handle her anger, but he was surprised to realize how much the thought of facing her disappointment disturbed him. A few weeks ago he would have longed for her to dismiss him, to send him back to Washington. He shook his head; the woman beside him was partly responsible for the change in his feelings. The rest of it—he wasn't sure. "Let me talk to the president first. If we can find the intruder ourselves . . ."

"If she doesn't know already, she will soon," Cat persisted. He dropped his hand; immediately she missed the comforting heat.

"Dammit, I'm responsible for the problem, Cat. Let me have a chance to solve it."

Catriona experienced a qualm about leaving the entire situation in his hands. Clearly there were still a lot of things about the community that he didn't approve of or believe in. Finally, however, she relented. "Okay."

They went to Cat's house and he called on the president's private line. He read out the names and furnished him with the scant information they had been able to gather.

"I'll get back to you tomorrow," the president said when Beck had finished.

"Yes, sir." He hesitated.

"Don't worry, Beck. I'll think of some way to accomplish this without involving your community. We wouldn't want to establish contact before you're ready to provide the information I want."

Beck's eyes flicked to Cat, then away. He knew with a sinking feeling that something had made her suspicious. "I know you will, sir. I'm not worried." Not much, he added to himself. He replaced the receiver and stood there with his hand on the instrument, as though maintaining contact would help him retain a measure of control.

Catriona had stood quietly to the side, watching and listening while Beck talked.

Now suddenly she couldn't look at him any longer. Something was going on, she knew it by the guarded glance he'd given her. She turned away and went to the pantry. "Would you like a soft drink?" she asked.

His hand fell away from the receiver. "Yeah."

The first hissing sound brought his gaze to her. He shook his head as she popped the top on the second can. "I'm still amazed every time you do that."

She gave him a wan smile. "From your side of the conversation, I gather that all we can do is wait."

He took the can she held out to him. "Thanks." Mentally he counted off the seconds before he took a swallow of the chilled drink. "He said he'd call in the morning."

"I hope he can help."

Beck finished the drink and tossed the can into the bin for recycling. ''Well, I guess I'd better get back to the greenhouse.'' He hesitated as though he were about to add something.

Catriona avoided his eyes. *Don't say it. I don't want to know,* she pleaded silently.

At last he sighed. She watched him go, her expression dull with apprehension. Surely he hadn't betrayed them. But his expression had been cautious as he'd talked to the president. There was something he wasn't telling her.

The next afternoon they walked side by side toward Elena's cottage, lost in their own thoughts.

Beck was feeling down for a lot of reasons. He'd tossed and turned in his attic bed last night, wishing he could explain everything to Cat. Wishing he could go back to the moment when the president had asked him to gather information about the community. He wanted her to understand.

He'd had to struggle to keep himself from going to her again in the wee hours of the morning. Even now he could picture her with perfect clarity in her bed, her hair spread out on the pillow, her beautiful body with its elegant curves and flawless skin, its shadowed places.... He bit off a groan.

''Good afternoon,'' Elena said from her chair under the ginkgo tree. Her cheerful voice brought them both out of their reverie.

They returned her greeting and joined her. Catriona settled into her usual spot on the grass at Elena's feet. Beck stood rocking slightly on his heels and looked down at the two women.

''We don't have much time left before winter comes. I decided to sit outside.'' She glanced from one of them to the other. "It looks as though the two of you have something on your minds."

"Yes." As she spoke Catriona glanced up at Beck, then away. This was his show. She would let him explain.

"Elena, I have bad news," he said bluntly.

Catriona frowned, irritated by his curt tone. Elena was an old woman. Couldn't he have led up to the subject more gently?

She sighed to herself. No, that wasn't Beck's way. She should understand by now that with him there would no skirting the issue, no wandering around to get to the point. He'd go straight for the heart of the dilemma.

"I have revealed the secret of Shared Ground to an outsider," he confessed.

Elena responded with a lift of her brow. The expression was so like Beck at his most superior that Catriona almost winced.

"You have?" Elena inquired calmly. She didn't seem surprised.

"And now we are in deep trouble."

"Go on," said Elena.

"I discussed the community with the president." He smiled with self-denunciation. "After he recovered he naturally had quite a few questions and I didn't hesitate to answer them all."

Elena nodded. "I can understand your feelings. You trust him absolutely."

"Yes, well..." He swung away, raking his fingers through his hair. "I found out that we were overheard by another member of the president's staff. And now, the man has sent someone to infiltrate the community."

Elena continued to sit quietly, hands folded in her lap, surprising Catriona. Didn't the old woman recognize the dangers in this situation.

Catriona looked up at Beck, who wore a puzzled frown to match her own. Suddenly a creeping feeling of disquiet, a feeling that had nothing to do with the spy, penetrated her consciousness. Elena should be thinking hard, she should be searching for a solution to this problem.

Catriona had watched her search; she knew the signs. She'd seen them often enough—a furrowed brow, tension in her shoulders, eyes narrowed in concentration—but none of those signs was present. Not one.

Beck went down on one knee beside his grandmother. He took her hand. When he spoke again, it was with quiet tenderness. "Let me explain further. As you know, there have been three new arrivals in the community since I've returned. I have had the president run security checks on the men, but he has been unable to come up with any clues as to which man is here under false pretenses."

Elena put her hand over her grandson's. Her smile was gentle. "You shouldn't have bothered. Don't look so worried, my dear. I assure you everything is as it should be in Shared Ground."

The slack-jawed expression on Beck's face would have been humorous if the situation wasn't so grave. "Elena, this man knows about the compound. He must know, too, about the stone."

Catriona inhaled sharply, filled with a dreadful premonition. Her nails dug into her palms. The other two ignored her. *Oh, God.*

"Beck," Elena said patiently. "The stone is secure. And the formula cannot be used for another two generations at least."

"You don't understand. We've got to find this man. We have to identify—"

She patted their clasped fingers reassuringly as she interrupted, "Of course, I understand," she said lightly. "It is you who do not. You haven't quite grasped everything yet because you're still fighting your heritage, Beck." She smiled serenely. "Don't you and Catriona have work to do?"

Beck's expression was poignant as he rose. He smiled and there was love in the smile. "Yes, we do. If you'll excuse us?"

"Of course," said Elena with a regal nod of her head.

He held out his hand to help Catriona to her feet. Their eyes met and held; they both recognized with sickening clarity that Elena was unfit to grasp the seriousness of the situation. He didn't release her as they both said a quiet goodbye and left his grandmother sitting relaxed and tranquil under the golden tree.

Catriona kept her churning emotions in check until they rounded the gate and were out of sight. She had known it would happen someday but... *Not now, please, not now.* Blinded by her tears, she stumbled.

Beck caught her when she would have fallen, steadied her and then he took her into his arms and held her. There was no need for words.

At last Catriona's tears subsided. Beck tilted her face up to the sunlight and wiped her cheeks dry with his thumbs. "Don't cry, Cat. She wouldn't want that."

She pulled out of his arms and sniffed. "Don't talk about her as though she were dead," she said.

"Face it, honey. Elena is almost one hundred years old. Like most others of her age, her mind has grown clouded. You've worried about that happening and so have I."

Though she agreed, she couldn't bear to hear him put the thought into words. She turned away from him and sat down on one of the nearby benches, wiping her tears away with the heel of her hand. "Have you? Have you really worried about her?" As soon as the words were out, she regretted them.

Beck stood looking down at her, his expression grim. "I'm not thoroughly heartless, Cat," he said distantly. "Elena *is* my grandmother. I may not have agreed with her in the past—"

"So what happens after we find the spy?" she interrupted. "Will you give the community the whole year you promised? Or will you use this as an excuse to leave?"

"You're perfectly capable of assuming leadership, Cat. I wish you would accept that. You have the brains, the experience."

"That's not true and you know it."

"It is true." He spoke slowly, and his deep voice had taken on a new timbre, as though he were exploring his thoughts as he spoke. "Elena's gift, as you call it, may be an asset but it is the determination of the people of Shared Ground that makes the community important."

The situation weighed so heavily upon her heart that she had to clench her fingers together to keep them from shaking. He was saying things that she'd told herself many times, but now that Elena seemed to be slipping, now that the time for decisions had arrived, she was frightened. What would happen to Shared Ground? What would happen to them all?

Beck wouldn't be staying; that was a certainty. Suddenly she needed to get away by herself. She rose. "I'll see you later." She turned to leave but was stopped by his grasp on her wrist.

"We still have a major problem here, Cat."

She didn't want to admit that she couldn't cope right now but he seemed to know anyway.

"We have to keep trying," he said with more gentleness in his tone than he'd shown thus far.

She shook her head. "I really don't give a damn about the spy. You handle it. I have other worries, much more important than one stupid little man."

"What the hell is more important than keeping the compound a secret? Do you want to lose control totally? Do you want the whole world trying to exploit your community?"

She whirled on him. "Without Elena—or her heir— there *isn't* a community, Beck. Aren't you and your boss planning an exploitation of some kind?" His expression sent her heart up to clog her throat. "You needn't bother to lie about it."

"I wouldn't think of lying to you," he said woodenly.

"The community, as we've always known it, will die. Someone will open Shared Ground up to the world. The people have always looked to your family for leadership. Their loyalty has been impressive, don't you think? And they believe—I believe—the only way to maintain the life-style is to use the Gardener's power."

"I don't agree with you, Cat. A compromise would work. The isolation of the community has given Shared Ground a reasonable amount of control over itself and its environment. There are millions of people who yearn to live like you do. You could set an example for them, show them the way.'' He hunkered down in front of her, every line in his body tensing to convince her of his sincerity.

"You are afraid of the outside world, but I'm not. We can show people that there is a way, a place where honesty and integrity are still considered virtues, where if people are encouraged to let their imagination roam free, without having to worry about crime and drugs and greed, they can come up with some extraordinary solutions to the earth's problems.''

Every word he said was like a wound to her heart. He still didn't understand. Her thoughts were frantic, unsettled. She couldn't argue logically because her reasoning was all tangled up with Elena's apparent confusion. "We can't pass a law to keep people out of Shared Ground. The subtle methods we use won't work forever. If we don't have superior leadership, our population will outgrow our resources.''

"Not if we don't let it.''

"We?'' she said sarcastically. "You've made it quite clear that you don't feel any responsibility for us. Well, I may not have your talents, but I do care. Maybe you're right, maybe disclosure is a foregone conclusion. If it is, I have to think about what I can do to save a part of this dream, anyway.''

Shocked by her stinging accusation, he dropped his hand and watched her walk away from him.

Chapter 13

Beck didn't approach quietly, but Catriona was aware of him even before she heard his footsteps, saw his long shadow.

She had turned to her own remedy for worry. She was on her knees, mulching her private vegetable garden.

The bulk of the shadow reached her side. She brushed the soil from her hands and stood to face him. There was something different in his expression, something she couldn't define, something she'd never seen there before, though she'd had a glimpse of it during the past weeks.

The only way she could explain the quality to herself was that he looked larger. His khaki pants and white shirt were pressed and fit him just as neatly; but, inside them, he seemed to have grown, as though the smooth fabric and starched creases could hardly contain his vitality, his confidence.

"I have come up with a plan that may smoke out Henderson's spy," he announced.

"Come inside," she said. He followed her into the kitchen and watched as she rinsed her hands and dried them on a tea towel. The knees of her well-worn jeans were covered with mulch and she wiped at them, too. Then she folded the towel carefully, as though the fate of the world depended on aligned corners. When she realized what she was doing, she flung the towel aside and turned her back to the sink, planting her hands on the counter behind her. "What's your plan?" she asked.

He massaged the back of his neck for a minute. Then his hand dropped to his side. "I want you to help me circulate a rumor."

She deliberately kept her expression bland. "What kind of rumor?"

"I want you to put out the word on the miracle alkaloid compound."

"Wh-at?" she asked, shocked. "We can't do that."

He waved away her protest. "You don't have to be specific or even declare its actual existence. Just drop a few hints that a breakthrough drug might be in the formulative stage. Let people know that you're excited about the potential and that we're working around the clock on its cultivation." He hesitated. "Put out the word that I'm going to be working in the experimental greenhouse for the next few nights. I want them talking about this thing," he added grimly.

She got the point and it raised her hopes. "Set a little trap and hope it catches your rat," she mused thoughtfully. She glanced at him, smiling a bit. "Is this what your friends in Washington would call a stakeout?"

"Exactly."

She shook her head. "It's too dangerous, Beck. For one thing, Elena would never go along with the idea of trying to trick anyone in Shared Ground. For another, the very existence of the compound is a secret."

"We wouldn't tell Elena," he said bluntly. "And as for the secret getting out, all we need is a hint. Henderson will have told his man to look for anything out of the ordinary."

"I like it," she said after a minute. "He won't be able to resist winding up his assignment. I know just where we can set it up, in the lab. We'll be waiting for him. Let me change my clothes and we'll get started."

Her animated reaction had brought a half smile to his face, but as she started to brush past him, he caught her around the waist. "Not 'we,' honey," he told her easily. "Me."

The hand at her waist was big and warm. She was tempted to lean into it. But she stepped back and he let her go. "Don't be impractical, Beck. Everyone knows you're my student."

"I don't want you in on this, Cat. I led Henderson's spy to the community and I'll be the one to get rid of him. We don't know what his instructions are, to what extent he will go to accomplish his mission. We don't even know he isn't armed. It could be dangerous."

"Your way is *more* dangerous, Beck, because it's a variation from the norm. Don't you see? I would never let you work alone in the lab. You're good but not that good yet. Besides, you're a pretty big man. This spy might not risk tangling with you. Let me be the bait. I'll work at the lab table in front of the window, just as I always do. It isn't unusual for me to work late. We can hide you somewhere, maybe in a closet."

"No."

She argued for another hour before she finally convinced him that he couldn't accomplish this without her cooperation. He wasn't happy with her plan. In fact, she observed with some amusement, he was downright uncivil. But at last he agreed, provisionally, as long as she went along with certain conditions.

The second night of their vigil was drawing slowly to a close. There had been no sign of anyone, not even indication of unusual interest on the part of any individual.

They had carefully gone over the details of their plan to smoke out the infiltrator. Their success had depended on the phrasing of the rumor and Catriona's ability to be convincing. They had thought they were offering the unknown man an attractive lure, one he couldn't ignore.

"Did you remember to leave the light burning in your room?" asked Catriona.

"Yes."

With a broad stroke of luck, they had reasoned, their man would take the burning light to mean that Beck was working or reading in his attic room at Elena's house.

Now, they were both ready to acknowledge defeat. Neither of them was particularly fond of spending long hours with busy work.

Catriona sighed her disappointment. "Maybe we didn't word our rumor strongly enough. Maybe the man didn't believe us."

"Either that or this guy is shrewder than we gave him credit for being. Or something has happened to prevent him from accepting our invitation," Beck muttered. "He only needed a suspicion," he added.

Oddly he wasn't as worried about Henderson's man as he had been two days ago. He couldn't explain the reason; perhaps during the long hours spent watching, he'd developed a fatalistic acceptance.

What the devil was wrong with him? Was his grandmother's condition contagious? There seemed to be this—not a voice, but some sort of presence—in his head that calmed and soothed him each time he thought about the infiltrator. He was beginning to wonder if he was making a fool of himself.

He was also beginning to feel like a stale pretzel. He didn't want Cat more than an arm's length from him, so he'd folded himself under the counter of her lab bench. The position was cramped and uncomfortable.

But the view was good.

These past two nights had been tantalizing, seductive and frustrating as hell. She was standing before the counter; he watched as she shifted from one foot to the other. He could see her only from the waist down, but he had no trouble imagining the rest. Occasionally, when she got tired of standing, she would use one sneaker-clad foot to pull over a stool and sit for a while.

A small smile grew as she shifted again. She placed the toe of one sneaker on top of the other.

Beck readily admitted to himself how much he'd missed her. After they agreed to set aside their animosity in the face of the threat, there had remained an initial wariness to overcome; but soon they were enthusiastically sharing their ideas, talking as freely— though in whispers—as they had when he'd first arrived.

Now he also admitted to himself how much he wanted her. One night, making love under the stars, wasn't enough. He was beginning to wonder if a lifetime of nights would be.

They'd been separate—together, but apart—from the moment she'd said she needed to shield herself from her own feelings. It was an encouraging excuse, full of promise, but he'd tried to give her the time and space she'd asked for.

The past two nights, however, had placed him in a sexual and emotional quandary. During the long hours, he'd begun to picture all the ways he wanted to make love to her—in a warm summer rain, before a fire while winter storms raged outside.

He knew now that love was a mild and colorless word for what he felt for Catriona. But he couldn't reveal his feelings; it wouldn't be fair to her. Not as long as he remained under an obligation to the president.

"It's almost four-thirty. I'm beginning to wonder if Elena was right, Beck."

He shifted away from his thoughts. "About our man? Yeah, me, too. She swore she hadn't turned thumbs-down on anyone, but I'm beginning to wonder if she even..." He let the rest of the statement go with a shrug.

"Remembered? Me, too. Oh, Beck, I hope we're wrong. I feel very strange about laying a trap. It goes against everything Elena has always taught me."

"Elena has never faced a situation like this."

"I know."

Suddenly they were both frozen by the sound of footsteps on the gravel path outside.

"Careful," warned Beck. His senses were suddenly alert, his quandary forgotten.

Catriona didn't need the warning. Her palms were sweaty, but she kept her expression reflective as she bent to the microscope, adjusted her focus. She made a note in the spiral binder on the counter beside her.

She felt an uncomfortable itch between her shoulders. Someone was watching.

When the knock came, she looked over her shoulder to see Brom Cunningham's large form through the glass panel of the door. Brom. Damn. She knew how much Beck liked the man. She pretended bewilderment but not alarm as she tossed the pencil aside and waved him in.

"Hi, Brom," she said, relieved that her greeting sounded negligible even over the thrum of her pulse in her ears. "What are you doing out at this time of night?"

He remained at the threshold. "I couldn't sleep," he explained calmly.

Her apprehension faded. If Brom was the spy and made the slightest move against her, Beck would be on him in a flash. But somehow she couldn't picture that.

He looked tired and troubled. Catriona felt a surge of sympathy, compassion even, for the man. She didn't know whether he was their spy or not, but clearly something was bothering him.

"I was wandering around in the garden and saw your light," he added. "Can I do anything to help?"

"No, thanks. I'm almost through here." She made a show of smothering a yawn, though she'd never felt more awake in her life.

"Then I'll leave you to your work." He started to back out the door.

Beck touched her leg. She knew exactly what he wanted. He might as well have been whispering in her ear. *Don't let him leave. Try to get him to open up.*

"Is something on your mind, Brom?" she said quickly and kindly. "Would you like to talk?"

He seemed to take the longest time to answer. "No, I don't think so, Cat." He'd picked up Beck's nickname for her. "Good night."

Beck heard the door latch click. The footsteps faded away. He muttered an expletive.

Cat's hands were at her sides, her fingers curled tightly in consternation. "I'm sorry," she whispered.

"Don't be sorry," he said immediately.

"I guess I'm not very good at this."

He understood her feelings. He felt the distaste, the aversion for what they were doing.

And suddenly he wanted—needed—to hold her. Desperately.

She shifted her stance from one hip to the other. He looked at the wrinkled fabric of her jeans. "Drop something," he ordered huskily.

"What?" Her fingers relaxed.

He repeated his command.

Catriona wasn't sure what Beck was planning. Perhaps he'd heard something in Brom's tone that she'd missed. She looked around nervously before she let her elbow brush against her notebook. When it fell, she followed it down. "What is it?"

Suddenly she was hauled into his lap. His mouth covered hers hungrily, moved on to trace her eyes, her beautiful cat's eyes, with kisses. "I hate this," he was whispering. "I hate it for me, but I hate it more for you. You are a beautiful, loving woman. You're right—you aren't cut out for deception."

She reached up to hold his head still and smiled into his eyes. "Neither are you," she said softly.

"As of this minute we're quitting, giving up this stupid idea. Dammit, Cat, Cunningham is my friend!" His expression was belligerent, but the anger was directed at himself. "I feel as though I have done something obscene tonight."

"Beck, no—"

Beck hugged her. "I'll talk to Elena, try to get her to take the problem of Henderson's spy more seriously. I'll explain my plan to her and admit that it was a flop."

He looked down at Cat, lying snugly in his arms, as though she belonged there. He'd known some scary moments when Brom walked in, wondering how and if he'd completely misjudged the man. "But you and I, honey, are finished playing James Bond."

Catriona heard the hard edge to his voice and understood immediately. He was blaming himself for suspecting Brom without proof. Most people could accept making a mistake, could even learn from one, but Beck, like his grandmother, would suffer over an error more than an ordinary person would.

From a society where distrust and doubt were established early in life out of necessity, where suspicion was a learned part of the psyche, like moodiness or depression, he had returned to Shared Ground, where trust and credence were a part of community life. Maybe Beck had come home at last. And maybe he would stay, in spirit if not in body.

Without warning, she felt a rush of love and empathy erase all her disquiet over their personal relationship. Without uncertainty, she felt an overwhelming, elementary urge to comfort him, no matter what the consequences might eventually be to herself.

She reached up to trace his heavy, scowling brows with her fingertips. "What time is it?" she asked with a drowsy smile.

He took her hand in his, placed his lips in her cupped palm. "It's almost five. Why?" he asked, though she suspected he knew the answer.

"Will you spend the rest of the night with me?" she asked in a low voice that set off a tingle in his spine. "I want you very much."

What might have been encouraged by regret and remorse quickly turned to tenderness and passion as they walked slowly to her house. They had barely crossed the threshold before he began on the buttons of her blouse and she was tugging at his shirt. By the time they were halfway up the steps they were naked.

Catriona giggled, feeling wonderfully wanton. She darted up the rest of the steps.

Beck caught her at the top, swept her into his arms. "Where?" he asked.

"Through there." She pointed.

He paused at the door to her bedroom and grinned at the sight. Her clothes were strewn from the dressing table chair to the window seat. "That first night, when I saw your house, I thought you were too neat."

She laughed, remembering that night as well as he. "'Perfection'?"

He chuckled and, crossing to the unmade bed, he dumped her on it. He stood there looking down at her, his smile fading with their laughter. Moonlight streamed in through the window. Like a blessing it coated her with silver light.

Moving slowly, he put a knee on the mattress, depressing it. "Well, maybe not in your housekeeping. But I've never seen anything as perfect as this." His voice had grown hoarse. She was all soft flowing lines. His hot gaze followed his hands as they moved over her with painstaking thoroughness, tracing every curve, convex across her breasts, and concave at her waist and throat, every bow, every arch, every turn of her body until he could have sculpted her shape from touch. "My beautiful, beautiful Cat," he whispered.

She raised her shaking hand to his mouth; her fingers were soft against his lips. "Beck." The word was an appeal, her voice thick with desire.

He covered her with his body, easing inside her, marveling anew at the way they conformed to each other.

The rhythm of their love gained strength and momentum until he began to drift, disembodied from reality. In desperation he clung to his control, leashing his spirit, until at last, he felt her shudder with tiny quick explosions, and he let go.

He felt her breath, warm and soft against his neck. He listened to his own heartbeat and knew that the remarkable miracle that had begun on the berm in the garden continued. Their lovemaking somehow transcended the scale of all human emotions.

And he knew that in a lifetime, a hundred lifetimes, nothing could ever be as exquisite as this. He could feel himself smiling as he slid toward sleep.

The chill of autumn was definitely in the air the next morning, Beck noted as he made his way to Elena's soon after eight. But though he wore the same short-sleeved shirt he'd had on yesterday, he barely felt the cold. All he had to do, he thought, grinning to himself, was think of his beautiful Cat.

She had offered to come with him, but this was something he had to do on his own.

He waved to a few people who were on their way to work and observed a chubby little boy of nine or so with amusement. Late for school and breathing hard, the child scurried down the road, book bag slapping his thigh.

A soft rain had begun to fall when he reached his grandmother's cottage. He pushed his hand through his damp hair as he entered through the front door.

In the kitchen Janet was setting a platter of pancakes on the table. Elena was in her seat. They looked at him in surprise, then Janet quickly looked away while Elena kept her gaze on him.

On the previous morning he had returned from the stakeout before Elena had awakened, before Janet had arrived. There had been no need for explanations, even if he'd been asked for one.

He hid a tired smile. Shared Ground wasn't a morally rigid community, but the people did retain the appearance of traditional values. "Good morning, Elena. Smells good, Janet."

Janet smiled bashfully. "Good morning," Elena answered with a confused frown.

When he and Cat had come up with the idea of setting the trap, he'd deliberately tried to block his thoughts from Elena, not knowing whether it would work or not. Apparently it had.

He joined her at the table and they ate in silence. When they had finished, Elena placed her napkin on the table and started to rise.

Beck finished his last swallow of coffee. "May I talk to you, Elena?"

"Certainly," she answered after a moment's hesitation. She led the way to her study, where a fire was blazing cheerfully on the hearth in deference to the nip in the air. They settled in wing chairs on each side of the hearth.

Beck wasn't looking forward to this conversation, but the only way to put it behind him was to begin. "Elena, I want you to think carefully about what we discussed the other day, the man sent from Washington to discover the secrets of Shared Ground. Do you remember?"

"Of course, I remember. And I told you not to worry about the man."

"Elena...Grandmother." He realized this was the first time since he was a child that he'd called her this. It felt right to him. "Grandmother, I don't think you're totally mindful of how serious this is," he said gently. "I know that you're getting older. We all do. And you mustn't feel that you've failed. You simply overlooked something. We have to find what you missed. And I want you to know that I'm here to help you."

Suddenly Elena sat up straight, her jaw sagged, her eyes widened in stunned surprise. "You blocked me!" she yelped. "You blocked your thoughts about the man. I thought you were doing it because of your love affair with Catriona."

He looked rueful. "I wasn't sure I could, but I didn't want you to worry."

"Worry?" She settled against the back of her chair, shaking with laughter.

He watched her from under lowered lids.

Finally the laughter subsided. She took a hankie from her pocket and wiped her eyes. She shook her head, but her mouth curved up at the corners. "I am deluged with joy, my cherished grandson. Do you realize what you have done?"

Beck frowned. "I haven't done anything. I just made an effort to keep from thinking about you."

"You blocked your thoughts from mine, Beck MacDomhall. You can no longer deny that you have the gift."

He scowled. "I do deny it," he said firmly.

She went on as though he hadn't spoken. "And if you can accomplish blocking, you can do more. You can receive thoughts."

He felt exasperated and helpless to do anything about it. "Elena, for God's sake—"

She raised her hand, effectively stopping his protest.

She paused, her eyes darting back and forth, as though she were reading an invisible book. As he watched, the amusement faded from her face to be replaced by annoyance. "You can begin testing your talent by focusing your attention first on your so-called infiltrator," she snapped testily.

Beck ignored her anger. He leaned forward, his elbows on his knees, his hands dangling loosely, and looked down at his shoes. How could he convince her?

He steeled himself and opened his mouth to speak, but when he met her gaze, sympathetic now, he felt an odd lassitude descend upon him. His spirit seemed to be fading as readily as the mountain mist faded under the noonday sun. He knew what was happening to him. No matter how vehemently he'd tried to deny the power, no matter how valiantly he'd fought against the knowledge, there was not—never had been—an avenue of escape.

He knew a need to conserve every atom, every particle of strength against this sudden pressure. His shoulders bowed as though pushed down by a huge, unseen hand; his head dropped.

Everything—his energy, his vigor and endurance, his vitality, his very substance seemed to be draining from him, like water drains steadily from a cup, leaving only a few last drops to fall.

His voice was low, almost a whisper, as he protested one last time. "Grandmother, I don't want this," he said, his voice husky with desperation.

Elena's eyes filled with tears. She rose and came to him, wrapping her arms around him. "I know, my dearest one. I know." He rested his head against her breast. "The magic of Shared Ground is a burden, but it is also a godsend. Relax now, relax and let the gift fill you."

"No." Alarm struck him like a dash of cold water. He pulled free of her arms. "No, I will not accept this."

He got to his feet shakily.

"Beck, don't. Please, don't."

He turned to look at her once more and saw her tears. But he couldn't let them move him. "I have to," he said, and left the room.

I have to fight this. Moving like a man in a daze, he stumbled to the front door and wrenched it open. It hit the wall with a hard crash. *I'm strong. I've fought it for years. I can fight for a while longer.* His thoughts were agitated, turbulent. But his energy was almost gone. Dizzy, groggy, almost mindless, he stumbled out into the rain.

He reached the forest. Moving from tree to tree, he made his way along the path to the belvedere. His gait was stiff and awkward, like a child learning to walk. Or a drunk.

At last he reached the lookout. Here he would be safe; here he could regain his rationality, his sanity. He leaned heavily against one of the pillars, breathing in huge harsh gasps that hurt his ears.

His knees gave way; he was sitting on the ground, his head back against the wall. He looked toward the sky, a rectangle of light gray framed by stone.

The misty rain stopped, and a cool breeze bathed his face. His breathing and his heart rate slackened, and clean mountain scents reached his nostrils.

He closed his eyes.

The last drop fell from the cup. He was empty. He had no idea how long he sat there. It might have been seconds or hours.

Slowly, gradually, the turbulence within him eased, tranquillity settled in his heart. He felt like a youngster again, surrounded and comforted by the warmth of his mother's arms, his father's strength.

Suddenly deep inside him, a spark flickered to life. It was only a glimmer at first behind his lids, as though from a distant candle in the blackest night, then it grew to a steady glow.

Mesmerized by the sensation that he was seeing, feeling, touching the warmth, Beck was completely unaware of his surroundings. The light grew brighter and stronger until it illuminated every corner of his being.

He breathed deeply. The light seemed to bring with it the return of his energy, his strength, magnified elevenfold. He opened his eyes and saw a rainbow painted across the rectangle of azure sky.

He knew himself, from what he had been from the moment of birth to what he would become. The phenomenon was both ominous and exhilarating.

Cat. He had to see Cat—to be with her. He needed her. Now.

He didn't know he had spoken aloud until he heard the echo of his own voice.

And his grandmother's. "Yes. Go to Catriona. She should be the first to know. Then you both return to me."

He left the belvedere and plunged into the sundappled forest, his stride purposeful. He wanted to run, to race to Cat's side! He felt he could even fly if he took a notion to!

But he was aware, too, that he needed the few minutes it would take to absorb at least part of what had happened to him or he was going to scare the hell out of Cat. When he reached her door, he didn't pause but walked right inside. He took the stairs two at a time.

Catriona was coming out of the bath, a towel wrapped turban-style around her head, her robe clinging to her damp body. "Beck," she said, startled by his sudden appearance. "What—was she very angry?"

He came to her and pulled her into his arms, lifting her and turning. "She was very angry," he said, setting her on her feet.

"Then why are you so happy?" she asked, confused by his grin.

Then she saw his eyes. Saw the glow reflected in their depths.

"Beck," she gasped. "You've—" She broke off.

Suddenly she was terrified. She wanted to flee; instead she hid her face in the front of his shirt, postponing the moment of discovery.

But Beck would have none of that. He would wipe the fear from her eyes, he vowed. He cupped her chin and made her meet his gaze. "Cat," he said softly, covering her lips with a warm, tender kiss. "Cat."

Without another word he lifted her in his arms and carried her into the bedroom.

This time, when they made love, it was a seal on their feelings for each other. He caressed her with infinite tenderness, enduring devotion. And when they scaled the heights together, they remained aloft for an unbelievable, magical time.

He held her to his heart, they dozed, but at last they had to return to the present. "Elena wants to talk to us both," he said into her hair. "Get your clothes on, lass." He gave her a playful swat on the bottom.

He talked the whole time she was dressing. On the way back to Elena's cottage, he continued to talk. The more things he said, the more afraid she became. But she kept a smile on her face.

"God, Cat, we all have the most fantastic future ahead of us. Shared Ground is going to make extraordinary strides in the next few years. We're going to give the world unheard-of gifts."

"The world outside?" she asked, aghast at the thought of opening the community to all the things they'd tried to protect it from for so many years.

"We'll retain a certain amount of isolation, but there are things we have to offer that must be shared. The things we've learned about protecting the environment, the energy resources, the food experiments, the nutrients you've developed. We will have to find a way to divulge them."

And what about you and me? How will you have time for me and the rest of the world, too? She scolded herself for the selfish thought, but she couldn't put it out of her mind, either. She only hoped he was too preoccupied with his newfound gift to read her mind.

As soon as they entered Elena's cottage, Beck took charge. Catriona noticed that Elena deferred to him in all decisions without hesitation. She evidently was confident that he would now make his permanent place in the community.

Catriona wasn't at all sure.

He'd talked of the many things that had to be accomplished, but how could he do them all from here? He had magnificent plans, but the mechanics of the expansion had to be worked out and what better place than the nation's capitol? It was central, well-known, the leaders of the world were comfortable there.

Besides he hadn't said he was staying. Catriona tried to pretend that her enthusiasm equaled theirs. She added her ideas to those put forth by Elena and Beck.

Beck only vetoed one plan of his grandmother's, and that veto added another layer to Catriona's doubts.

Elena wanted to inform the community that Beck had fully developed his gift. It was a cause for celebration, she insisted.

Beck hedged, looking extremely uncomfortable—at least in Catriona's eyes—as he explained to Elena that it was imperative that he return briefly to Washington. There was still the matter of the president's aide, he rationalized, the one who had sent Brom to Shared Ground. The man had to be dealt with. There was also the matter of Beck's vow to the president.

Catriona feared, deep in her heart, that Beck would never return from Washington. Not for good anyway. The responsibilities he would face there would build until he realized that he would be more effective in the nation's capital. She hid her melancholy from them both.

"How long will it take you to pack?"

The question brought Catriona out of her reverie with a jolt. "Me?" she said.

"Of course, you," he said with a grin that was a challenge.

He knew how much she hated to leave Shared Ground. He seemed to be daring her. Did she have the strength, the courage to match his?

"Surely you don't think I'd leave you behind?" he went on. "I'd like to get as far as the interstate highway before dark."

She set aside her hesitation. This was a reprieve, a little more time to spend with him. She looked to Elena, who nodded. "Yes, go with him. You can catch up on your sleep while he drives."

"I can be ready in half an hour," she told Beck, her mind already skipping ahead. She'd have to reset the thermostat in the tropical greenhouse, get someone lined up to check on...

Beck touched her cheek. "I'll hurry," she told him breathlessly.

When Cat had left, Elena turned to Beck. "Honestly, I can't understand why the two of you didn't trust me. Could it be that you thought I was growing senile?"

He smiled. "I'm afraid that's exactly what we did think."

"Well, now you know better."

"Yes, ma'am."

"Sit down." The mellowed woman who had been in evidence for the last few hours disappeared. Elena was suddenly all business again. "Most of the things we have to discuss can be postponed until you return, but there are one or two items to decide upon before you go. Such as: what things are we willing to share, and how can we be protected."

He listened to her, interrupting only occasionally to have her clarify a point, while she spoke. Her happiness, as well as her relief that she finally had someone to share the burden of leadership, shone like a beacon from her clear blue eyes.

As they talked, he realized there were many facets to the gift that he didn't understand yet. But that would come with time.

At last Elena interrupted herself. "I don't know why I'm rattling on. You had better get packed yourself. Catriona should be ready soon."

He rose and bent to kiss her wrinkled cheek. "I'm ready," he said, and she knew that he didn't mean his suitcase was packed. She smiled and walked toward the stairs with him.

When they reached the banister she stopped him with a gentle touch. "The man you called the infiltrator? You know who he is. Do you understand about him now?"

He covered her hand with his and smiled. "Yes, I understand. Brom was never a danger to the community, because he had become a part of Shared Ground almost immediately after he arrived."

"He's a fine young man. You have a lot of things in common."

"I don't understand why he didn't come to talk to me when he knew he was going to stay. I would have trusted him."

"Maybe he wasn't sure he trusted you."

For a fraction of a second Beck was confused. When he did comprehend her meaning, he almost wished he hadn't. "You knew that the president wanted me to collect information about the community and take it all back to Washington."

"Yes, I did."

Beck looked away from those blue eyes toward the top of the stairs. "I'll talk to Brom when I get back."

"You do that." She gave his arm a last pat. "I think you and Brom will be good friends."

Chapter 14

Cat was asleep on the seat beside him. Beck glanced over with an affectionate smile. He himself had never felt less tired in his life. It was as though he'd found a way to personalize and draw upon those boundless resources of energy. He had reached the outskirts of Washington in the small hours of the morning and driven to his house.

He pulled into the driveway, turned off the motor and waited.

The suspension of noise and movement woke Catriona. She yawned and stretched, then looked around her. "We're here? I can't believe I slept the whole way, Beck. Why didn't you wake me?"

Smiling slightly, he tucked a strand of hair behind her ear, then he laid his hand on her cheek. "Maybe I felt heroic, standing guard while my lady rested."

His fingers were warm on her skin. She covered his hand with her own, holding it to her cheek. It was quiet and dark and they might have been alone in the world. "Chauvinist," she taunted in a tender voice.

"Probably," he agreed in a low, sexy growl that turned her bones to butter. "Let's go inside and find out."

They made love in the bed and again in the shower. As the sun rose in the east, they were bundled in thick terry-cloth robes, sitting double in a single chaise longue on his patio, sipping hot coffee. They watched the first few flakes of snow begin to fall.

Comfortable in the curve of Beck's arm, Catriona cupped the warm mug in both hands and inhaled the fragrant brew. "This is crazy, you know. It's nearly wintertime and we're outside in our bathrobes."

He set his own mug aside and added his other arm to the embrace. "There. Are you cold now?"

She looked up into his eyes. Her smile was playful. "I wasn't cold before. I was simply making an observation about the status of our sanity."

"Let me see." He buried his lips in the curve underneath her hair. Her skin was warm and slightly damp and she smelled like his soap. "Yep," he chuckled. "You're warm there." He maneuvered his mouth to her throat. "And there." He began to tug on the belt of the robe.

"Beck, we really will freeze. Stop."

He sighed with mock resignation, released one arm and reached for his coffee. "You're a formidable woman, Catriona Muir."

"It would take a formidable woman to deal with you, MacDomhall."

He grinned, loving her so much that keeping his mouth shut was almost painful. He wanted to tell her, but he felt that he had to extricate himself from his promise first. When he pledged his love and his life to her, it would be with a clean slate between them. "Right. You'll never let me rest on my laurels, that's for sure."

His words spoke of a future for them, a future Catriona still didn't believe in. He would remain here in Washington, while she would return to the community. She couldn't live like that; she simply couldn't. She felt a stinging behind her eyelids and dropped her chin.

He raised it with a finger. "Cat, honey? Is something wrong?"

"You mean you can't read my mind?" She sounded playful, a lot more playful than she felt. "That's a relief."

Beck looked at her for a long minute. He was very serious when he spoke again. "It's odd. I think I could if you'd let me. But for some reason I can't."

"Good," she told him. "It wouldn't be a bit fair." She decided to give him an opening. She shrugged. "You know me, Beck. I'm never completely comfortable outside Shared Ground."

He didn't take the opening she offered, and she felt her heart sink another notch. She sat up and swung her legs off the chaise. "We'd better get dressed, Beck." She hesitated. "That is if you still want me to go with you to the White House."

He frowned, seemingly inclined to continue the discussion, but finally he relented. "Of course, I want you to go with me."

They entered the kitchen. The telephone rang then, and that was the last she saw of Beck for two hours.

Beck showed her to a reception room near the president's office and promised to return shortly. "As long as I'm here, I need to check in on a few things. You understand, don't you, Cat?''

"Of course." She leaned over to pick up a magazine. "I'll be fine," she said briskly.

He reappeared seventy-five minutes later, full of apologies and looking slightly harassed. "Sorry I took so long, honey. The president's ready to see us now."

The Oval Office was just as she had expected it to be from the pictures she'd seen. The room was beautiful, dignified, and yet not at all intimidating. The snow, which had begun at daybreak, had continued, and now a blanket of white lay over the famous rose garden. Dormant now, the bushes would be beautiful when they began to bud and blossom in the spring.

The president stood beside her, looking out through the French doors. He knew of her interest in growing, living things, and he had talked to her of some of the other interesting plants on the White House grounds. "You'll have to come back when everything begins to bloom, Catriona," he suggested.

"I would love to see everything in bloom," she said quietly.

"And so you shall," he promised.

But Catriona wondered if she would ever see this town again. She also wondered if it would be best if she left now, as soon as this meeting was over, if she went away before she could be sent away.

"Now, let's get down to business," said the president briskly. He sat behind the large desk, and they took chairs across from him. "Beck, what have you found out about Henderson's man?"

Beck filled him in on Brom Cunningham. "He's decided to stay with us, sir. And as a member of the community he's not about to reveal what he's discovered."

The president's face took on a worried frown. "But there's still the matter of Roger Henderson. We haven't been able to locate him."

Beck cleared his throat. "Well, sir, I have had some thoughts on that."

The president nodded for him to proceed.

"The physicians who treated you are taking the credit for your recovery, Mr. President. They are the finest doctors in the country—in the world. Who would believe a crackpot who told a story about a miracle cure? If Roger went to the media with this, he would look like a fool, don't you think? Only you and I, and Cat and my grandmother even know about the formula for the alkaloid. Not even the residents of Shared Ground know more than a rumor of it."

"But Shared Ground is a secret itself. If Roger goes to the media, they'll begin to nose around."

"And they would find a rather nice, progressive small town in Tennessee. No different from many other towns where the leadership is trying to solve their problems—improve education, clean up the environment. At least for now."

"What does that mean?"

Beck relaxed in the chair. He straightened his legs and crossed them at the ankles; he linked his fingers over his stomach and said thoughtfully, "Sir, I have convinced my grandmother that our isolation is not as practical in today's world as it was when our ancestors settled in the mountains. There are some startling technological advances that I am anxious to look into further.

"Also, Cat and her staff are doing some really breakthrough work that I feel we should share. They've developed nutritional bonanzas that are years ahead of anything I've ever heard of. Fruits and vegetables, genetically altered and tailored to an individual's medical needs. Cat will explain further in a report.''

Catriona swung her head around to stare at him. This was the first she'd heard of a report.

''We have things to share with the country, sir. Politics aside, these things have the potential to make life better for a lot of people.''

The president had listened thoughtfully while Beck spoke to him of the potential of Shared Ground. Now he nodded and opened his mouth to answer. But he was interrupted by a light blinking on his phone.

He gave Catriona an apologetic smile. ''I'm sorry to have to postpone the rest of this, but my secretary reminds me that I have another appointment.'' The light blinked again, impatiently.

Catriona rose as the president lifted the receiver. ''Just a minute,'' he barked to whomever was on the other end.

He held out his hand to her. ''I'll look forward to receiving a report about your findings, Catriona,'' he said. ''And don't forget, you're coming back to see the gardens in the spring.''

Catriona smiled, murmured a goodbye.

He added, ''Beck can you hang around for a few minutes?''

Beck nodded and went with her to the door of the office. He gave her arm a squeeze. ''This won't take a minute,'' he said, then gave her a rueful grin. ''I hope. Sorry, honey.'' He showed her out and shut the door behind her.

Doubt rose in Catriona's eyes as she looked at the blank door, wondering why in the world he'd brought her with him. He would never be free of this place, nor would he waive his connection with it. She glared at the door to the sanctuary, the room that was the seat of power.

And suddenly she couldn't blame Beck for wanting to remain a part of the excitement, the electricity. This was his niche, and his job fulfilled his needs, just as the garden fulfilled hers. She thought of the last time, a few days ago, she had walked the gravel paths, wandering with no direction in mind, simply absorbing the peace and beauty of the place. Yes, she could understand his wanting to stay. But it wasn't for her.

Behind the door the president was asking, "What are your long-range plans, Beck? Are you going to keep your word to return to my staff? Or do you mean to stay in Shared Ground even after the year of commitment to your grandmother is over?"

The man was never one to beat about the bush. Beck inhaled, filling his lungs in preparation for a disagreement.

Instead the president went on, "Hard as this is for me to say, if you decide not to return to Washington, I want you to know I'll understand."

Beck let the breath out on a hearty sigh of relief. He hadn't expected it to be this easy. "Thank you, sir. I thought you would. I seem to have acquired responsibilities at home that I hadn't expected."

"I need you here, too, you know."

"There is a greater need there. And a greater potential," Beck said gently. And he knew, in his heart, that Shared Ground was where he really belonged, where he could serve his country best.

"From the things you've intimated, I'm inclined to agree with you." He paused and shifted a paper on his desk. "I had already begun to feel guilty about asking you to gather information on your community."

"I felt uncomfortable, too," admitted Beck.

They grinned at each other. Then the president sobered. "Have you worked out a way to maintain confidential communication between us?"

Last night, during the long ride, Beck had done a lot of thinking. "I've thought about using Brom Cunningham as a liaison, if that meets with your approval. And his. Brom has the experience and the expertise to explain the technological achievements of the community. More than I do, at this point. So far, I've been working exclusively in the garden with Cat. That will change now. My responsibilities will be broader. But I want you to know, sir, and my grandmother agrees, I'll return to Washington temporarily, whenever you need me."

"I'm relieved to hear that. As much for the country's sake as for my own." The president chuckled. "What are you going to do if I'm defeated next election?"

That possibility hadn't occurred to Beck. He thought for a minute. A smile spread across his face. "You won't be," he said softly.

The president looked puzzled. "Well, we won't have to worry about that for a couple of years, anyway. And if you live as long as your grandmother, the country will have another sixty-odd years of your service."

The older man rose and came around the desk. Beck stood to face him, swallowing a thickness in his throat. He was saying goodbye to an important part of his life.

The two men clasped hands, held on. "You've been like a son to me for many years, Beck," said the president. "I'll miss you."

"I'll miss you, too, sir."

* * *

Beck entered the corridor outside the Oval Office and looked around for Cat. The president's appointments secretary looked up. "The young lady left, Mr. Mac-Domhall."

Left? Why would she leave? "Did she say where she was going?"

"No, sir."

Beck frowned. Maybe she was outside. But when he reached the door, there was no sign of her. The guard at the gate told him she'd hailed a taxi.

Beck muttered an imprecation under his breath. He couldn't understand why Cat would do something like this. He'd been preoccupied this morning and had left her alone, but surely she wasn't sulking because he'd had business to attend to. It wasn't like her to sulk, period.

He drove to his house as quickly as the traffic allowed. But the moment he walked in the door he knew, without looking, that she wasn't there. Where the hell *was* she?

He knew dread. And fear—she was uncomfortable in the city. God, if something happened to her, he'd never forgive himself. He looked around, blindly searching, as though suddenly finding himself in an alien environment.

A sound from the driveway spun him around and back down the hall to throw open the front door.

A taxi was pulling away. Cat stuffed her wallet back into her purse, muttering to herself about worthless cab drivers taking advantage of unsuspecting tourists.

"Where the hell have you been?" he roared to hide his relief. He met her at the foot of the steps and clamped down hard on her shoulders.

She looked up at him with a chilling self-possession. "I got the cab driver to stop at a travel agent's office."

Beck was truly perplexed. "What on earth for?"

"For a plane ticket."

"Cat, maybe I'm stupid, but I don't understand." He shook his head. "Would you like to explain?"

She sighed. He could feel the slight trembling in her body through his hands, but he wouldn't have known there was anything wrong if he hadn't been touching her. Her chin was lifted to a stubborn angle. And he had no idea what her thoughts were.

"Beck, I know you want to stay in Washington. I don't blame you. But I can't live in endless suspense about our relationship." She bent her head. "And right now, I just want very badly to go home."

"We'll go tomorrow. Won't you wait for me?"

"I can't," she said in a whisper.

"Cat, look at me." The hoarse tone of his voice more than his command brought her eyes up. She gasped at the pain she saw in his gaze. She stepped toward him.

"None of this, not the gift, not my job, nothing would be important without you by my side. Nothing! Don't you see, Cat? I love you more than anything in the world. I want you to be my wife."

"Aren't you going to stay in Washington?" she asked softly, not willing to believe, not yet.

"No. Why would you think that? I told the president we were leaving tomorrow."

"I thought he would convince you to stay," she said, hating the weakness in her voice, but loving the glow of happiness that had begun to grow in her heart. "Beck, I can't read your mind," she said with some asperity.

"I can't read yours, either. But I'll tell you this. I'm going home to Shared Ground. It's where we both belong and nothing would keep me from you. I love you," he said again. "Oh, God, Cat. I love you."

"Oh, Beck," she cried, moving forward into his strong arms, arms that wrapped securely around her, arms that would hold her forever. "I love you, too."

A week later Catriona walked in the garden, but this time she had a definite direction. The people of Shared Ground had gathered near the Chinese willow tree to witness the marriage of Catriona Muir to Beck Mac-Domhall. The tree's branches were bare, but there were other trees, evergreens and pines, as a backdrop for the small white kneeling bench.

The sacred words, the vows, the kiss, and then it was done. They were man and wife.

His gaze met hers. For a breathless moment the crowd was motionless, waiting. Then Beck laughed out loud, the sound filled with exhilaration. He took Catriona under his arm and turned with her to face his grandmother. "Elena, your granddaughter."

She smiled. "Catriona has always been that." She leaned forward to kiss Catriona's cheek. "But welcome to the family, officially, my dear."

Elena's part in the celebration was cut short in deference to her age, but the wedding party would last long into the night. Beck and Cat sneaked away to see Elena back to her cottage. "Good night, Grandmother," said Beck when they reached her door.

"Come in," she said. "I have a wedding present for you. It will only take a moment."

They followed as she led the way to her study. She sat down behind her desk and opened the drawer. From it she took two envelopes made of parchment. She held them up so that Beck and Catriona could see that they were sealed with crimson wax. Then she placed them on the desk in front of her.

"The strength and effectiveness of our valuable secret alkaloid is synergism, a total that equals more than the sum of its parts. The strength and effectiveness of your marriage will be governed by the same principle. I am giving you each half the formula for the compound to make a significant point—that each of you is strengthened by your union. And the strength of Shared Ground will rest on that solidity and your leadership." She turned to her grandson. "There will be many occasions when you must defer to Catriona."

Beck was amused to notice Cat's startled expression. He reached for her hand and gripped it tight.

"There is another job which is yours to fulfill. You must find a geologist to study the stone."

He felt his heart leap in anticipation. But that could wait. "Grandmother, you're being premature. You hold on to those envelopes for a while."

Elena smiled. "I don't intend to retire completely, my dear. But I am turning the major portion of the responsibility for the formula, and for the community, to you and Catriona. I have held on long past my time.

"After tonight, the community will accept both of you as Gardeners. With my blessings." She placed her hands on the arms of her chair and levered herself to her feet. "Now, go and enjoy yourselves."

She allowed them to kiss her cheeks and then they left.

"Oh, Lord, Beck. Can we do it? Can we really manage all the responsibility that's going to come with opening up to the world?"

"Together, my love. Together, we will," he promised.

And, thought Catriona, who should know better than the MacDomhalls?

* * * * *

FOUR UNIQUE SERIES
FOR EVERY WOMAN YOU ARE...

Silhouette Romance ®

Tender, delightful, provocative—stories that capture the laughter, the tears, the *joy* of falling in love. Pure romance...straight from the heart!

SILHOUETTE *Desire* ®

Go wild with Desire! Passionate, emotional, sensuous stories of fiery romance. With heroines you'll like and heroes you'll *love*, Silhouette Desire never fails to deliver.

Silhouette Special Edition ®

Stories of love and life, these powerful novels are tales that you can identify with—romances with "something special" added in! Silhouette Special Edition is entertainment for the heart.

SILHOUETTE·INTIMATE·MOMENTS™

Enter a world where passions run hot and excitement is the rule. Dramatic, larger-than-life and always compelling—Silhouette Intimate Moments will never let you down.